A

W9-APU-431

DEAD OF SUMMER

Books by Mark Miano

Flesh and Stone

The Street Where She Lived

Dead of Summer

Published by Kensington Books

DEAD OF SUMMER

MARK MIANO

Kensington Books
http://www.kensingtonbooks.com

KENSINGTON BOOKS are published by

Kensington Publishing Corp.
850 Third Avenue
New York, NY 10022

Library of Congress Card Catalog Number: 98-067477
ISBN 1-57566-404-6

First Kensington Hardcover Printing: April, 1999
10 9 8 7 6 5 4 3 2 1

Printed in the United States of America

For Mom and Dad

One

The cottage looked exactly as Michael Carpo remembered it from previous summers: the gray clapboards baked in the midafternoon sun; the chimney jutted serenely from the roof, like a tall dormant volcano; and the three front windows reflected various angles of the rental car as he rounded the final turn in the driveway. It was only after parking outside the garage that he noticed what looked different about the cottage this year: The front door was open.

He unbuckled his seat belt, waited for the dust to settle, then stepped out. The engine pinged from the heat of the two-hour drive, radiating a furnacelike blast against his bare legs. Somewhere in the woods a crow yapped, but Carpo's eyes never strayed from the cottage. The door fluttered in the light breeze, back and forth, as hesitant as a butterfly wing. It made him frown.

Something felt wrong about the cottage. Something more than an open door that had been overlooked. It was Jack Crawford, or, more precisely, the lack of him that so deeply worried Carpo. Jack always came to the door to greet his houseguests.

Carpo was familiar enough with the cottage to barge inside, but out of respect for Jack he stayed at the entrance and knocked. Then he leaned inside and yelled: "Hello, Jack? You home?"

Only Floyd responded, Jack's big, old black Lab. The dog had been named after Floyd Patterson, the former boxing champ, but when the dog heard Carpo, he howled like a terrified pup. Carpo entered the house immediately, tracing the barks down the foyer, through the book-lined living room, to the bathroom. This time the door was closed. Carpo knocked on it once, turned the knob, and found Jack.

He was sprawled on the floor, arms spread wide, palms up, as if he had been crucified to the ceramic tiles. His body floated on a sea of ruby red, a thick, glistening current that circled his outstretched arms and his splayed legs, and created a nearly perfect halo around his head. These red waters flowed from a deep well: two jagged gashes hacked into each wrist. He looked as if he had bled nine of his ten pints.

A scream rose in Carpo's throat, a strange choking noise that he had never made before. It took him a second to comprehend what he was seeing, and when he did, a white flash exploded in his eyes, so bright and intense that it brought him to his knees.

"My God, Jack, what have you done?"

He scrambled across the floor, through the blood, and cradled the head in his arms. He shook it, then slapped its cheeks, then pounded its chest. It wasn't Jack; Jack was gone forever.

Every August, Jack traveled for one week to Athens, Georgia, to visit his sister and her family. While he was away, Carpo looked after the cottage. He answered the telephone, collected the mail, watered the gardens, and fed and exercised Floyd. In exchange, he got to spend a relaxing week in the country, far from the hot, crowded sidewalks of Manhattan, in a place psychologically light-years from Channel 8 News, where he worked frenetic ten-hour days as a television news writer and field producer.

Jack lived in Bridgewater, Connecticut, a sleepy town of twelve hundred people nestled in the southern part of Litchfield County. During the 1980s the region became fashionable with "weekenders," wealthy Manhattan professionals drawn to the lush countryside, the quaint farms, and the enormous white colonial homes, some that actually dated back to the Revolutionary War.

By comparison, Jack's house was modern and modest: a small two-bedroom cottage built in the 1950s on a steep valley that overlooked Lake Lillinonah. Inside, the cottage had the dark, stuffy feel of a gentleman's club: overstuffed leather furniture, dusty Persian rugs and walls covered with oil paintings, watercolors and black and white photographs. The living room had an enormous walk-in fireplace and bookshelves lining three of its walls from the baseboard to the ceiling. This fortresslike chamber of wood, stone, and bound paper was contrasted by the fourth wall: a large bay window that afforded a view of the lake.

It was to the living room that Carpo retreated after calling 911. He waited on the couch, body rocking with anxiety and revulsion. A sickeningly sweet odor had filled the cottage, attracting a swarm of houseflies. He put his hands over his ears to clamp out their unholy buzz, but he didn't have the stomach to get off the couch and close the bathroom door.

My God, Jack, my God, he thought over and over. *Why have you done this to me?*

Finally, a car rolled down the driveway. The engine stopped, a door slammed, and footsteps lumbered up the flagstones. A Litchfield County state trooper appeared in the doorway, his profession betrayed by the distinct silhouette of his Smokey the Bear hat. He stared into the house, blinking in the darkness, until he spotted Carpo.

"There was a report of a suicide here?"

Carpo rose unsteadily. "Yes, sir."

The trooper removed his hat and stepped inside. He was a big man; six two or three, maybe 250 pounds. He had red hair shaved to the scalp; longer strands of red sprouted from his neck, wrists, nostrils, and knuckles.

"Where is it?" the trooper asked.

"What?"

"The suicide."

Carpo pointed at the bathroom. "In there."

The trooper crossed the room. As he passed, Carpo got a glimpse of the name on his silver badge: TROOPER B. WALKER.

Trooper Walker stared into the bathroom for a minute. Without turning he asked: "Who is it?"

"Jack Crawford." Carpo wished the trooper were facing him so he could see if he recognized Jack's name.

"Does he live here?"

"Yes, sir."

After a few more seconds Trooper Walker stepped back. He turned to Carpo and an immediate change came over him, his chest relaxing, the stiffness dropping from his shoulders. He shook his head and exhaled with a loud *whoosh,* as if to say he was sorry.

Another set of tires scratched the driveway; it belonged to a blue minivan with mirrored windows and a dent in the grille. Three men piled out of the front: an older man dressed in an out-of-season tweed blazer and two younger men wearing tight black T-shirts with the word MORGUE printed in yellow letters across the chest.

Trooper Walker excused himself. He huddled in the driveway with the new arrivals, conversing out of Carpo's earshot before they filed into the cottage. The older man nodded politely at Carpo, then slipped into the bathroom, closing the door behind him. He stayed there for a long time, ten or fifteen minutes. Trooper Walker and the morgue workers spent the time reminiscing about their last suicide calls. Carpo did his best to ignore them, sitting alone on the couch, head buried in hands.

When the older man reappeared, he nodded at the others, then walked to Carpo and dangled a hand in his face. "How do you do, son? My name's Dr. Singer. I'm the coroner for this end of the county."

Carpo accepted the hand in silence. Singer glanced about for a seat, then flopped beside Carpo. No sooner had he settled into the leather cushion than he began peppering Carpo with questions.

"What's your name, son? Michael Carpo? We ever met before, Michael? No? 'Cause you look sort of familiar to me. How old are you? Thirty? Now, I'd have guessed you were no more than twenty-five. Where you employed? Channel 8 News? So you're a city cat, eh? What do you do for the news? A writer *and* a field producer? Then I'll bet you've seen a body before this one, eh?"

On and on the questions came, in a voice several decibels

louder than normal. Carpo responded to the first few questions, but he found it difficult to follow them. After a while he stopped trying. Singer didn't seem to notice, pausing just long enough to make up an answer, pass an opinion, or fire a new question. The assault was so intense, Carpo began to feel light-headed. He couldn't fathom what Singer was doing, blabbering so loudly and inconsiderately, until he heard Jack Crawford fart in the bathroom, as loud as a trumpet blast.

Singer may have looked and acted like a bumbling country coroner, but Carpo felt a sudden surge of respect for him; he knew his job, and knew it well. He was sitting in the living room, jabbering away, hoping to prevent Carpo from hearing just that sort of noise. Carpo trained his ears past Singer's voice, onto the bathroom. He heard rubber-soled shoes squeak on bloody tile, and grunts and whispered curses as the morgue workers struggled with the weight of the dead. He also heard sounds from Jack: moans, farts, wheezes, and sighs. Sounds animate enough to make him sit up on the couch and think, *Jack's still alive!*, even though he had seen firsthand the vacant stare in his face and the gashes in his wrists, wide enough to slip two fingers through.

The last noise from the bathroom made Carpo shudder: the menacing screech of a zipper being closed, meaning that Jack was going inside a body bag. Feeling sick, Carpo got to his feet. "I need a drink."

"You go right ahead, son."

In the kitchen Carpo rummaged through the cabinets until he found the bottle of Maker's Mark. He poured a large shot into a juice glass and knocked it back, eyes pressed as the liquid scorched his throat. When the burn cleared, he forced another down, then he wiped the tears from his face and waited for the bourbon to start working.

The kitchen had been Jack's favorite room in the cottage: a bright, airy space with cherry-wood cabinets, a solid oak butcher block, and a cathedral ceiling. Jack had done the finishing work on the cabinets himself, and, like a set of fingerprints, they still displayed his unique touch: a door sawed a quarter-inch too short; a pane of glass cracked by an errant hammer blow; two drawer knobs whittled from wood after the brass ones had run out. The entire cottage was like that, everywhere an imprint of Jack, everything a reminder to Carpo.

Carpo dumped ice cubes into the glass and soaked them with a healthy quantity of honey-colored bourbon. He carried it to the living room just in time to catch Dr. Singer nosing through the papers on Jack's desk. When the coroner realized Carpo had returned, he bolted upright. "I'm just looking for the phone."

Carpo pointed at the unit next to the couch, in plain view. Singer avoided making eye contact as he picked it up and dialed a number. Carpo sat at the desk, placing his glass on a marble coaster beside the Smith Corona typewriter, the same typewriter on which Jack had hammered out hundreds of newspaper columns, fourteen novels, three biographies, and an autobiography.

His first summer at the cottage Carpo had fantasized about using the typewriter to compose something for himself—a diary, an essay, or perhaps even a short story. The machine was electric, an ancient, oversized model that hummed with power and leapt around the desk every time the return key was struck. But when the big moment arrived, the typewriter proved to be more of a distraction than an inspiration. He spent most of his time straightening the base and the rest flexing the kinks out of his knuckles after pounding the hard, round keys.

Carpo rubbed a hand across the keys now, his thoughts interrupted by Dr. Singer; he was asking someone where he should deliver Jack's body. The question seemed odd to Carpo, especially since the coroner had arrived with two morgue employees, so he asked about it once Singer was off the phone.

A grin spread across the coroner's face, a chastising smirk that suggested Carpo shouldn't be listening in on people's private conversations. "You see, Mike, these fellows come from the Danbury morgue. My office is in New Milford, and I usually bring my own crew, but our van's at the garage, having repairs. So now I've got to find out who's got jurisdiction over your pal, New Milford or Danbury."

The explanation made sense to Carpo, even though the flip reference to Jack irked him.

Trooper Walker emerged from the bathroom, hands protected by a pair of yellow gloves with a raised daisy flower design; he peeled them off from the wrist down, to capture the wet blood. Next, the morgue workers emerged with the body bag, a long vinyl pouch that sagged in the center like a rolled carpet.

Dr. Singer smoothed out his pants as he mumbled something about notifying next of kin and funeral arrangements. Carpo felt numb. He watched them slide Jack into the rear of the van, then Dr. Singer and the morgue workers squeezed into the front seat and left.

Trooper Walker made a call on the radio in his squad car before he returned to the cottage. He slid into the rocker across from Carpo, the chair's wicker weave creaking as he struggled to undo the buttons at his collar. The T-shirt beneath was stretched to transparency by a jungle of red chest hair. When he was finally settled, he said, "If you're up to it, Michael, I'd like to ask a few questions about your friend."

Carpo closed his eyes and nodded. His face felt saturated with alcohol, eyelids swollen from crying. More than anything, he wanted to be alone.

"Tell me how you found the body."

"I drove up from the city this morning. Got here about an hour ago. The front door was open and when I called hello, Floyd started crying. That's how I knew Jack was in the bathroom."

"Who's Floyd?"

"Jack's dog."

"That's right, I saw the prints in the blood. Anyhow"— the trooper glanced around the room—"where's he now?"

Carpo looked around too, realizing for the first time that Floyd was missing. "I don't know. I haven't seen him since I opened the bathroom."

"Do you live here?"

"No, I'm here just for a week. I look after the house every summer while Jack visits his relatives in Georgia. He was supposed to leave tomorrow morning, first thing."

"You have a key?"

"Yes, but like I said, the door was open, so I didn't have to use it."

Trooper Walker scratched the hair trapped beneath the T-shirt. "When you went into that bathroom, did you touch anything?"

"I checked to see if he was alive."

"Did you remove anything?"

"No, sir."

Trooper Walker frowned. "So was it just business between you two? Or were you friends?"

Carpo leaned his head against the cushions. He wished that he could blink and—*poof!*—make the trooper disappear. *Were we friends?* He guessed the relationship could be described like that, though it didn't come close to explaining what Jack had meant to him.

"Yes," he said quietly. "We were friends."

"Did Jack mention anything to you about personal problems? Maybe he was depressed, or under pressure? Anything like that stick out?"

Carpo crushed an ice cube between his teeth; it tasted like diluted bourbon. *Did Jack foreshadow his suicide?* he wondered. They had last talked two weeks before. Jack had phoned him in the newsroom to ask what time he'd be arriving in Bridgewater. It was part of their ritual; the first night of the week, Jack would prepare his famous "eight-by-eight marinated pork chops." Carpo returned the favor a week later, on the night of Jack's return, by barbecuing some steaks on the grill. During their last conversation, Jack had given no hint of a problem. He hadn't complained about stress or depression. In fact, he hadn't complained about anything.

"We talked by telephone two weeks ago. Jack sounded fine. Just like he always did."

"How's that?"

"What?"

"How did he always sound?"

Carpo shrugged. "Gruff, mostly, I guess. Nothing to suggest he was thinking of this."

"So he was expecting you today?"

The way Trooper Walker asked it, the question sounded more like an accusation; Carpo nodded yes anyway. "Because I checked both cars in the driveway," the trooper continued. "I assume the rental's yours, right? So why isn't that Jeep all packed up with suitcases?"

"Jack wasn't leaving until tomorrow."

"You arrived a day early?"

"No, sir, I planned it that way. We had planned on eating dinner together tonight."

Trooper Walker rocked forward and stayed there, his eyebrows forming inquisitive red crescents. "It sounds like you and Jack were very close," he said with care. "Any chance that maybe you were, like, his boyfriend?"

Carpo's cheeks steamed, though he knew he shouldn't resent the question. The cottage was very small; living room, dining room, kitchen, and two tiny bedrooms. Not to mention that on the surface he and Jack appeared to have little in common, being of different age and different race. Odd as it all seemed, it wasn't the way they were.

"No, we were just friends," Carpo said, "Nothing more."

The trooper planted his feet and squiggled out of the chair. He placed his hat on his head, running his fingers along the brim to ensure its alignment. "How much longer you plan to be in Bridgewater, Michael? Just in case I need to ask you something else."

"I don't know yet. I was planning on staying the week. I guess I'll stick around until Jack's affairs are put into place."

The trooper pulled a business card from his shirt pocket. "Please call me if you think of anything else. And what about the phone here? Is it listed?"

"No, it isn't."

Carpo waited for the trooper to pull a notepad and pen from his back pocket, then recited the cottage's phone number. They walked to the door, stopping at the first step.

"If you have any problems with the press over the next few days, give me a buzz," Trooper Walker said. "I can post a man at the top of the driveway, keep things under control."

He stared hard at the trooper. "So you know who Jack was."

"I've heard of him. Never read his stuff, but I know he was pretty famous. Anyway, Bridgewater's no different from any other town. We're a bit smaller, but we've got gawkers and gossipers like everywhere else. If people start traipsing across the lawn, call me."

"Thanks, I will." He shook the trooper's hand. "By the way, when does Dr. Singer release the autopsy results?"

"This case, I doubt there'll be one. He examined the body here, ruled it clear-cut suicide. No real sense in dragging it out."

"But in New York the M.E. always autopsies a suicide. It's standard procedure."

"It may be S.O.P. in your city, but not in mine. I know it sounds strange, but that's the way we do things here. Doc Singer ruled it a suicide, and so it'll stand." Trooper Walker eased down the steps, backward, thumbs tucked in his gun belt. "Say, my wife runs a cleaning service over in New Milford. You want, I'll send her out here to clean up that mess in the bathroom."

Carpo waved off the trooper's offer. "Thanks, but I'll handle it. I need something to do over the next few hours. It'll keep me busy. I've got to keep busy."

Two

As the trooper's squad car turned the corner of the driveway and disappeared, an empty feeling formed in Carpo's stomach. The cottage felt quiet and desolate; he suddenly wondered if he had made a mistake by not accepting help from Trooper Walker's wife. But then he imagined how it would feel to face another stranger, someone inclined to ask him about Jack, the suicide, and what might have prompted it. With that in mind he felt reasonably sure that he had made the right decision.

He located the necessary cleaning products in the bathroom's walk-in linen closet: plastic bucket, liquid soap, and a plastic bristle scrub brush. He placed the bucket in the bathtub and filled it with scalding water, adding a capful of soap. He agitated the water with his hand to form suds and then used them to attack the crusted blood, still a silhouette of Jack. He wielded the brush with maniacal vigor, scrubbing the floor until the white tiles had reappeared at the surface.

By the time he was finished, the water in the bucket had a thin film of muck, like a still pond in the dead of summer. He dumped it behind the house in a patch of pachysandra. The last remnants of Jack lined the inside of the bucket: specks of blood that had been turned green by some ingredient in the cleanser. He rinsed it out with the garden hose and left the bucket on the porch to dry. The scrub brush was beyond salvaging, the bristles flattened and badly stained; he tossed it in the trash.

He retrieved his suitcase from the trunk of the car and carried it into the cool, dark house. As he walked through the living room, he began to see the interior with a different perspective, one influenced by his recent antiseptic outburst. Catching his attention first, the dust: long, sooty threads hanging from the roof beams and light fixtures like cobwebs; finer, gray particles coating the bookshelves and window-panes like powdered snow. It looked as if Jack had last dusted in 1956, the year the cottage was built. More than likely, it had taken place in 1973, the year that Effie, his wife, succumbed to ovarian cancer.

Carpo grabbed a rag from the linen closet, dampened it under the tap, and then ran it across every flat, dust-collecting surface within reach. Since the dust was heaviest around the fireplace, he spent extra time removing the various objects from the mantel and wiping them down.

Jack had been a notorious collector of what he called *chotchkes*. It took Carpo a few years to learn that *chotchke* was a real word, Yiddish for "useless collectible," which perfectly described the plethora of objects on the mantel: a brass rococo candelabrum that Jack had bought in a Mont-martre junk shop, three basalt arrowheads unearthed in the vegetable garden, a glass jar filled with multicolored beach glass, an old photograph of Jack in his U.S. Navy uniform, an empty Chianti bottle wrapped in straw, and a wooden pipe-stand that held a collection of smelly Dunhill briars.

The most intriguing object on the mantel was a polished

piece of wood about three feet high with a bulbous head carved into the shape of the letter C. The first time Carpo had seen it, he thought it was an abstract sculpture of a woman; the C denoting a mouth and the sloping angle beneath representing breasts. The object turned out to be a *forcola*, a hand-carved oarlock that Jack had purchased in a gondola repair shop in Venice. Ever the utilitarian, Jack had loved the idea that a basic tool could double as a work of art.

When the cottage looked as clean as at any time Jack had lived in it, Carpo went outside to call for Floyd. The dog had been missing since he had opened the bathroom door. Knowing how Labradors tended to wander, Carpo was starting to worry. He stood in the driveway for twenty minutes, hollering the dog's name and blowing a special whistle. Finally, Floyd appeared from the edge of the woods, head down, tail slinking between his hind legs.

Floyd came from the litter of two field trial champions, but he had grown too big for competition. He weighed more than a hundred pounds, with a broad, muscular chest and softball-sized paws. His fur was the color of coal, from the tip of his wet nose to the end of his tail; the only nonblack part of him were his sad brown eyes.

As the dog drew closer, Carpo noticed the spots of dried blood on his paws and chest; tiny russet pebbles that clumped in his fur. Carpo snared him by the collar and led him to the backyard, where he soaked him with the garden hose, using his fingers to scratch free the stubborn clumps. Down at his level, Floyd gently licked Carpo's cheek. As sad as Carpo felt inside, the sensation of Floyd's rough pink tongue brought a smile to his face.

Fur cleaned, Floyd took a step back and succumbed to a convulsive shake, the water spinning off his back like a lawn sprinkler. Carpo led the dog into the kitchen, refilled the water bowl, and tossed him a treat. Floyd ignored both as he walked through the living room, straight to the bathroom. The dog stopped at the door's edge, where pine wood abutted ceramic tile, and peered inside, almost as if he still expected to see Jack in there. After a bit, the dog began to whimper, a sound so mournful that Carpo began to cry himself. He walked to the dog and reached down to pet him. "It's okay, Floyd, it's okay."

But as soon as his hand touched fur, Floyd yelped and shied away. The reaction startled Carpo; he figured the dog was sad, but the response had been one of utter terror. Before he could react, Floyd darted under Jack's writing desk, leaving just the tip of his nose exposed in the shadows.

Carpo followed, getting on his hands and knees and crawling beneath the desk. He rubbed the dog's ears and scratched his belly until he got him to stop shaking. Within minutes the dog was slumped over his leg, fast asleep. He guessed the dog's response was due to the trauma of spending the morning trapped in the bathroom as his master bled to death.

The telephone rang. Carpo extricated his body from Floyd's and answered it. "Hello?"

The line was silent for five seconds, though Carpo could hear someone breathing on the other end.

"Hello? Is anyone there?"

"Ummm . . . sorry," a man said. "I must have the wrong number."

Carpo hung up the phone. No more than ten seconds

later, the phone rang again. This time, when he answered it, he didn't say anything.

"Hello? Is anyone there?" the voice at the other end asked.

It was the same man who had just telephoned. "Who's calling?" Carpo demanded.

"Is Jack Crawford home?"

"I asked who's calling."

There was a pause, then the man said, "It's Art Bengar."

"Where are you calling from, Art?"

"New York City."

"I figured that. I mean where are you from? Who do you work for?"

"I'm from *The Times*," the man said sheepishly. "I'm trying to verify a bulletin that came over the wires about a half hour ago saying Jack Crawford died. Can you confirm that for me?"

Carpo took a deep breath. Was he ready to deal with the media? Just three hours after Jack had died? Once he gave confirmation, he knew he'd have to deal with a blitz for the next few days. Was he emotionally ready for it?

"Yes," he said. "He died."

"Is it true he committed suicide?"

Carpo didn't answer, silently cursing Trooper Walker, Dr. Singer, and the morgue workers. One or all of them had tipped someone off.

"Hello?" the man asked. "Are you still there?"

"I'm here."

"I asked if it was true Crawford killed himself?"

"You're a journalist. Find out for yourself."

Before the man could respond, Carpo slammed down

the telephone. Then he unplugged the cord. It had been a miscalculation on his part; he was not prepared to handle the press.

The growl in his stomach reminded him that his last meal, a bagel with cream cheese, had been consumed more than six hours earlier. He headed to the kitchen and scoured the cabinets, taking stock of the food on hand.

Mostly, it was soup. Stacks of aluminum cans three deep lined the shelves of the cupboards, each row grouped by a different flavor or brand name. While the supply was ample, it was apparent that Jack had preferred one flavor: chicken. There were traditional flavors, such as chicken noodle, chicken and rice, chicken bouillon and cream of chicken. There were exotic stocks too: chicken chowder, chicken minestrone, chicken chow mein, and even something called chicken cheddar chunks. Jack used to believe that chicken soup made his digestive tract run smoother. Carpo didn't know if it was true or not, but he did know that Jack's sodium count had been in the stratosphere. Even after his doctor ordered him to go on a salt-restricted diet, Jack had insisted on eating a can of chicken soup for lunch every day.

"I'd rather be a goddamned dead man from high blood pressure than a constipated live one for cutting out my broth," Jack had once bristled when the subject of his soup intake came up.

Jack used to sprinkle his speech with liberal doses of a *goddamn*, *Jesus Christ*, or *chrissakes*. It could sound pretty intimidating to a stranger, but it never bothered Carpo. It added a level of energy and urgency to Jack's tone, as if everything he said—even a statement on soup intake—were a matter of grave importance. His writing had been like that too: not quite so profane, but a hearty, opinionated tone that made the articles, stories and books impossible to put down.

Carpo was looking for something more substantial than soup, so he moved to the refrigerator. He broke into an immediate grin when he saw what was inside there: two full racks of Piel's beer, identified by its short brown bottle and twist-off cap. Jack used to call the beer a "stubby" because the shape of the bottle reminded him of a stubby person's body. On impulse, Carpo grabbed one, snapped off the cap, and took a long drink.

His first summer in Bridgewater, Carpo had gone for a walk in the woods below the cottage. He had come across a faint dirt path winding through the trees and, thinking that it was a deer trail leading to the lake, had followed it. After thirty yards or so the trail had ended at a mound of smashed brown glass, almost waist high. It turned out to be the spot where Jack discarded his glass back in the days before Bridgewater offered regular garbage pickup. The size of the pile got Carpo wondering how many stubbies Jack had consumed in his lifetime.

"Of all the cockamamie questions, that surely is the cock-amamiest!" Jack had bellowed when Carpo put the question to him. "I've been drinking two stubbies a day since I turned seventeen. Hell, Mr. Piel himself ought to give me a lifetime supply, amount of money I've spent on that damn piss water."

At the time, it occurred to Carpo that no shards of Maker's Mark bottles existed in the pile. Knowing how Jack liked his evening tipple, Carpo had asked him where he had disposed of those bottles.

A wry smile had come over Jack's face as he explained:

"Effie didn't allow liquor in the house. Called it the devil's drink. No, I didn't discover bourbon until after she died. Imagine that, Carpo, all those years of teetotalism just to keep my pretty bride smiling."

Standing before the open refrigerator, a stubby in one hand, the cool air blowing across his knees, Carpo felt a surge of anger. Just thinking about Jack and his stories, and the goddamned way he used to tell them. It made Carpo wonder again: *Why did you do it, Jack? Why did you kill yourself? And why did you do it so I'd be the one to find you?*

And as if Jack Crawford were standing beside him, Carpo received an answer. It was on the bottom rack of the refrigerator in a pink ceramic bowl: four large pork chops seeping in a dark, oily marinade. Carpo's heart started knocking against his chest as he pulled the bowl out for closer inspection.

A layer of plastic wrap covered the bowl, but it couldn't contain the pungent aroma of Jack's famous eight-by-eight marinated pork chops. The name came from the recipe: eight hours of marinating followed by eight minutes on a blazing mesquite grill. The resulting chops were black and crispy on the outside and juicy inside, one of the most tantalizing, mouth-watering dishes Carpo had ever tasted.

The clock on the stove read five P.M., roughly two hours before the time he and Jack had planned on eating dinner. Carpo had arrived at the cottage at one P.M. If Jack had marinated the pork chops as the recipe called, he must have prepared them at eleven that morning, a mere two hours before Carpo had discovered his body.

What man planning to commit suicide would take the

time to prepare dinner for later that evening, a dinner for two that he should not have been expecting to eat?

Just by staring into that bowl, watching the meat bob in the dark mixture, Carpo realized that Jack had not planned on dying that morning. The hair on his neck became electrified as he thought: *Jack didn't commit suicide after all. Someone murdered him.*

Three

That night, for the first time in more than a year, Carpo dreamed of his father.

It took place in the house where Carpo had spent his childhood, a small split-level condominium in Roslyn, Long Island, a suburb of New York City. His father was seated at the dinner table, working a crossword puzzle. The room was very bright, as if illuminated by floodlight, and it was easy to see his father's face. He looked different than Carpo remembered: frail and old. Wrinkles had formed around his eyes, and white hair had sprouted at his temples and in his mustache. His hands trembled noticeably, the movement magnified in the curled edges of the newspaper. He seemed oblivious of Carpo's presence, studying the puzzle through a pair of half-sized reading glasses, occasionally jotting down an answer or erasing a mistake.

Carpo was seated in an adjoining room; the angle seemed to indicate the kitchen, but the lights were off and it was too dark to be certain. A thin wedge of light spilled from the dining room into his room, a solitary bridge that linked the opposing sides: light to dark, Carpo to his father.

His father looked so real to him, so alive and nearby that he tried to yell to him. But when he opened his mouth, his lips and tongue seemed to be paralyzed. He couldn't even muster a groan. He tried to stand and walk into the dining room, but discovered that he could not move, his arms and legs curiously immobilized or else bound so tightly to the chair that he couldn't even lean forward. All he could do was sit in the dark, silent and motionless, and watch his father through the doorway.

When Carpo awoke from the dream, he was drenched in sweat, but otherwise unsurprised that he had re-experienced this dream. After a day filled with such trauma and anguish, he had almost expected it. Jack's death—which he no longer believed to be a suicide—was the first tragedy to befall him since the day four years ago that he and his father had stopped speaking.

However, there had been a new element to the dream this time, something that had transformed it from a merely disturbing dream to a full-blown nightmare. Lying in bed, Floyd curled at his feet, he tried to remember what it was. Had he been able to call to his father? Or rise from the chair? Had his father spoken back to him? Try as he might, he couldn't remember. All he knew is that something had happened just before waking that had terrified him worse than ever.

At the first hint of dawn, he climbed from bed to brew a pot of coffee. He drank it on the screened-in porch, wrapped in one of Jack's scratchy wool sweaters. Down in the valley, Lake Lillinonah appeared as a jagged black line slicing across the purple backdrop of woods. As the sun took a firm grip on the sky, the valley and lake underwent dozens of changes in color. To Carpo it was like watching an artist mix paints: the dark colors turning lighter and more distinct as dabs of white, yellow, and blue were added to the palette. When the sky became streaked with cobalt blue, the steel bridge spanning the lake became visible.

Even with coffee, Carpo's eyelids sagged from lack of sleep. Feet on the table, warm mug clutched against his stomach, he allowed himself to drift off. The catnap might have turned into something substantial if it hadn't been for the strange noise that started in the backyard.

It came from the left side of the cottage, a sharp clicking noise that stood apart from the bird chirps, rustling leaves, and whimpers from Floyd, lost in the clutches of his own doggie nap. Carpo set his coffee mug on the table and went to investigate.

As he approached that side of the porch, the clicking sound changed from sharp snips into distinct metallic snaps. They emanated from the flower garden, a fifteen-foot-square plot surrounded with a chicken-wire fence to keep the deer out. A young woman stood in the center of the garden, walking down the aisle of rosebushes. Every so often she reached out and clipped the head off a flower. Nearly a dozen colorful specimens—red, yellow, purple, and white—packed her left hand. In her right she clutched the weapon: an oversized pair of garden shears. Its long, curved blades glinted with every assault on a flower stem; a split second later, the staccato report of metal striking metal reached the porch.

Carpo watched the woman for more than a minute, his body frozen with incredulity. He knew the countless hours Jack had toiled in that garden: planting, watering, weeding, fertilizing, and pruning, until the plot of dirt and manure had been transformed into a lush, colorful oasis. In fact, his reaction to the woman was much the same as Jack's might have been if he had caught an intruder beheading his prized flowers.

"What the hell are you doing?" Carpo shouted as he burst through the screen door and charged the garden.

The woman looked at him with a shocked expression, then dropped the garden shears, put her hands to her mouth, and screamed.

He halted when he reached the garden's border, his cheeks reddening. "I'm sorry, I didn't mean to scare you," he said, suddenly humbled. He couldn't help but soften his tone, finding himself face-to-face with a beautiful woman.

She was about an inch taller than he and slender, and she wore a pair of faded denim overalls that fell away from her body in places that made it almost impossible not to gawk. Sometime, long ago, her descendants must have traveled through Scandinavia; she had high cheekbones, a smooth cream complexion, and a pair of large blue eyes. Of course, that meant her hair was blond, and it stayed that way down to the root. She wore no makeup on her face, no jewelry on her body, no adornment whatsoever beyond the shimmering blond mane that draped her shoulders like silk taffeta. A bee the size of a Ping-Pong ball hovered near her face; she brushed it away as nonchalantly as if she were shooing a fly.

Carpo regained his composure. "Why are you cutting those flowers?"

"I'm picking them for my studio," the woman said as if it were the most natural thing in the world for her to be doing.

"Do you know Jack?"

"Yes, of course. We're neighbors. I live just up the road, on Skyline Ridge."

When the woman mentioned her home, she pointed the fist of flowers toward the woods. Carpo vaguely recalled a small cottage in that direction, about a quarter of a mile away. "I have some very bad news," he said, throat constricting. "Jack died yesterday."

"What?" The woman dropped the bundle of flowers, her lower lip trembling noticeably. "No, no, no, that's not possible. I saw him yesterday morning. Saw him right here. What happened? Did he have a heart attack?"

In spite of his own theory, Carpo thought it best to stick with the official ruling. "It seems that he took his own life."

"Jack killed himself? No way, I don't believe it. I *can't* believe it. He wouldn't do a thing like that."

She rubbed her knuckles against her lips, trying to force back the sobs. Carpo tried to think of something to say that would comfort her, but nothing came to mind. It was too late anyway. The sobs broke through, and the woman broke down.

It lasted a minute or two, though it felt much longer to Carpo. He stood with his head bowed, hands shoved deep in his pockets, jiggling keys and loose change, helpless and uncomfortable. When she finished crying, the tears remained behind, clouding her eyes and enlarging them, as if a tiny magnifying glass had been placed over the center of each cornea.

"Would you like to go inside?" Carpo offered. "I made some coffee."

She nodded, then gathered her flowers and garden shears. They walked to the cottage in silence, Carpo holding the screen door for her. He asked her to wait on the porch while he went for the coffee. The serving tray was under the sink; on it, he arranged the coffeepot, two mugs, sugar, milk, and a plate of oatmeal cookies. When he returned to the porch, the woman was on the wicker couch, legs curled beneath her body, Floyd nestled tight against her. The dog nudged her hand for attention, flipping it up on his head. Carpo noted the way she scratched him, rough and between the ears, just the way he loved it.

Carpo set the tray on the table, then sat across from her. "If he starts bugging you, just push him away."

"Floydie, he could never bug me, could you, baby?" the woman cooed, intensifying the massage.

Hearing the woman address Floyd by his proper name made Carpo feel better; it meant that she had at least known Jack. He poured two mugs of coffee and handed her one. She smiled and said, "Thanks," then added a drop of milk and two sugar cubes.

"My name is Michael Carpo," he said, extending his hand across the table.

"I'm Amanda Cutler." She grasped his hand. "I should explain why I'm here. I'm a painter, and Jack used to let me clip his flowers in order to make sketches of them."

Carpo suppressed the grin at his lips. Jack may have been as protective as a parent about his flowers, but he could never resist a pretty face.

"I'm a friend of Jack's from New York City. I've been coming here the past six years to watch the cottage while he was away."

"Yesterday, he mentioned you'd be coming. He was supposed to warn you that I might be stopping by."

They both fell silent, their thoughts returning to Jack. Carpo felt a sting of envy that Amanda had been able to see him one last time. He hadn't seen Jack since last August, an entire year ago. If only he had arrived at the cottage an hour earlier, maybe he could have done something, maybe even saved Jack from whatever had happened.

Under different circumstances, Carpo might have seen the irony in that thought since it was Jack, six years earlier, who essentially had saved him.

They had been introduced by Major Sisco, the executive producer at Channel 8 and Carpo's direct boss. At the time, Carpo had been covering a story about the murder of a prominent art dealer in Central Park. Carpo came under police scrutiny—and intense media interest—when a woman he had once dated became the prime suspect in the crime. After the case was resolved, Sisco arranged for him to stay with Jack in Bridgewater until the controversy died down.

Carpo noticed that the woman's eyes had filled with tears again. He leaned closer. "Amanda, can I get you anything?"

"I'll be okay in a sec." She dabbed a knuckle in the corners of her eyes. "I just can't believe it, you know? Twenty-four hours ago, I'm standing out there talking to him just like every morning, and now I'll never see him again. I can't understand why he'd do it. It's totally not his style."

"Believe me, I can't either. Did Jack say anything yesterday that sounded strange? Maybe he was upset about something . . . or someone?"

She stared over his shoulder into the woods, eyes unfocused. "No, he sounded fine. We didn't talk for a very long time."

"What time did you see him?"

"Sometime around eight."

"What did you talk about?"

"He told me about you. He asked me to make sure that you were having a good time. We would have talked longer, but someone pulled in the driveway." Amanda grimaced, shaking her head. "Isn't that ironic? The last time I ever saw him and I never even said good-bye."

Carpo's skin prickled. "Did you see who it was?"

"Who?"

"The person who pulled in the driveway."

"I couldn't tell. Jack said it was probably the Jehovah's Witness people coming to try and convert him again."

"How long did you stay after that?"

"No more than five minutes. I didn't want to hang around, in case it was company."

Carpo couldn't think of anything else to ask Amanda about the visitor, but he couldn't help wondering who had visited Jack right before his death. *Could it have been his murderer?*

Amanda picked up her mug and sipped. "Mmmm, coffee's delicious."

He grabbed his own mug and took a swallow. It *was* delicious, hot and strong like espresso, just the way he liked it.

Coffee was something of an addiction with Carpo. When he was working in the newsroom, he often downed ten or twelve cups in a single day. And he was picky about what he consumed: splurging for gourmet beans, grinding them by hand in his apartment, then brewing them in a special deluxe coffeemaker. This coffee had come from his favorite store in New York; he knew from experience that Jack would have only supermarket coffee on hand.

"What do you do, Michael? Jack said that you were a writer, but what type?"

"I'm not a writer, not a real one at least."

"What do you mean?"

"I write copy for the anchors at Channel 8 News."

"And that's not writing?"

"It's more like typing. Usually, I'm just regurgitating what's on the wires or in the newspaper."

Amanda's eyes narrowed. "You're just being modest. Jack said you were a wonderful writer."

"Jack said that?" Carpo asked, unable to conceal his surprise. It was an odd thing for Jack to say, especially since Jack had never read anything by him besides an occasional letter and, a few years ago, a short story. "How about you?" he asked. "You're a painter?"

"Yes."

"What's your work like?"

She sipped more coffee, then kept the mug near her lips, steam obscuring her eyes. "I do still lifes. You could call the style realist."

"You must be good if you can support yourself."

"I'm doing pretty well. I don't show in the city yet, but I'm hoping that will change soon." She set her mug on the table. "This area's gotten pretty trendy in the last few years, and it certainly doesn't hurt to be a local artist. About the only thing working against me is my technique. It takes me forever to finish something."

"Do you have a gallery? I'd love to see your work."

"Harold Jackson is my dealer. His gallery is in Kent. But

why drive all the way there to see it? Drop by my studio. I'd be happy to show you."

"Where is it?"

"In an old barn behind my house. Stop by anytime." Amanda shifted Floyd's head off her leg. "I should probably be pushing off, Michael. Thank you for the coffee. Do you know when there will be information about funeral arrangements?"

"I'm not sure yet." Carpo set down his mug. "I still haven't been able to notify Jack's family. I'm sure they're going to want his body shipped to Georgia."

"Well, please keep me posted. And call me if you need help with anything. Either way, I expect a visit from you later this week."

They shook hands, then Amanda gathered her roses and slid the shears into a narrow pocket on the side of her knee. Carpo walked her to the door and stood there as she headed up the driveway, her long blond hair and finely muscled shoulders leaving an impression on him after she had disappeared.

It was past nine o'clock, yet the grogginess still lingered behind his eyes; he felt as if his forehead was packed with cotton balls. He considered heading back to bed for a few hours to make up on missed sleep. Instead, he refilled his coffee mug and carried it to the porch, sinking into the wicker chair.

The nightmare was still knocking at his head, something about it bugging him. What was it? He stared into the valley, where the sun created millions of light flecks on the lake surface, trying to remember. When he did, he had to sit up in the chair to catch his breath.

The dream had started as it always did. His father was at the dining room table, working a crossword puzzle. He looked old and tired, but this time he was not alone. Joining him at the table was a second person, an elderly black man with a light gray afro and eyebrows that drooped in a permanent scowl that partly concealed his milky-white eyes.

It was Jack Crawford, calmly puffing on one of his putrid black stogies between sips off a brown-bottled stubby.

Four

Apparently, the word was out about Jack Crawford. By ten A.M. the cottage had received four more telephone calls from reporters, each one fishing for exclusive details of the suicide. Carpo avoided their questions by saying he was not a member of Jack's family, and therefore unable to comment. In truth, it burned him up to keep silent; it made him feel helpless, frustrated, as if he were betraying the memory of Jack. More than anything, he wanted to tell the press—and the world—what he now fervently believed: *Jack Crawford didn't kill himself.*

The final straw was the arrival of a photographer; Carpo never learned if the man was from a magazine or a newspaper. The intruder sat in his car with the doors locked and the windows up, snapping shot after shot with a high-speed film advancer. He ignored Carpo until finally Carpo charged the car with a fireplace poker, brandishing it around the windshield like a crazy man. The act must have looked convincing, because the man dropped his camera and sped away. The fleeing car left long black tire scars in the driveway. Carpo went back inside the cottage and walked from room to room, lowering window shades, drawing curtains, and locking doors. Then he climbed into the rental car, Floyd at his side, and drove for the center of town.

Route 133 was the main road to town. It was called a route because the state of Connecticut maintained it, but it looked the same as any other road in town: single white line down the center, potholes and bumps on the surface, and sides buried under a layer of sand and salt from last year's snowplows. Besides connecting New Milford to Brookfield, Route 133 also served as Bridgewater's unofficial main street. On the right he passed the volunteer fire department, the primary school, the town library, and the town hall. At the end of the stretch on the left, he pulled into a complex of buildings that housed the post office, the New Milford Savings Bank, and the Village Store.

In many ways, the Village Store was the centerpiece of town; a tall, ornate gingerbread building erected in 1899. Inside, the store retained a nineteenth-century country charm: jars filled with penny candy, walls decorated with pounded tin, and a warped wood floor that creaked from another era.

Carpo walked straight to the newspaper racks and grabbed copies of *The New York Times, Daily News*, and the local papers, *The New Milford Times, The Danbury News*, and *The Litchfield County Times*. He paid for them at the register, then stood beside the counter and flipped to each obituary section. There was no mention of Jack. Word may have gotten out about his death, but it had come too late to make the morning papers.

In the car he fished Trooper Walker's card out of his wallet, checked the address, then drove a hundred yards down Route 133 until he spotted the corresponding house:

a modern two-story split-level painted white to match the older colonial houses on the street. He continued down the road until he found a shady spot, in which he parked. He rolled down the windows for Floyd, who had jumped in the backseat for a nap, and proceeded to the house.

There were two entrances to Trooper Walker's house, a front door and a garage-side door. Carpo chose the front door even though it didn't look as if it got much use. The yard was unmowed, the shrubbery lining the foundation untrimmed, and the front walkway littered with toys—a plastic pirate's cutlass, a metal cap gun, and a brigade of little green army men. Carpo stepped over the toys and pressed the doorbell. A moment later Trooper Walker opened the door.

He was wearing his uniform pants but only a white T-shirt on top. The skin on his face glowed from a recent shave, so recent that dots of shaving cream lingered beneath his earlobes. He stared at Carpo through the screen door, hand on the knob. "Oh, yeah," he said, recognizing Carpo, "Jack Crawford's friend, right?"

"Yes, Michael Carpo."

The trooper nodded. "I was going to stop by your place today to see how you're doing, but now you've saved me the trip. Come in."

Trooper Walker held open the door, then led Carpo to a room with two rottweilers sleeping on the couch. The dogs must have smelled Floyd, because they hopped off the couch and swarmed over Carpo, shoving their noses into impolite places. Trooper Walker seemed oblivious of the molestation; he offered to make coffee, and Carpo accepted.

As soon as the trooper left, Carpo pushed away the dogs.

A large-screen television in the corner was playing *The Price Is Right* with the sound muted. A stack of gun and hunting magazines sat on the coffee table before him, and a series of pastel drawings of Indians hunting buffalo decorated the walls.

Suddenly, a woman padded into the room in a terry-cloth robe and sheepskin slippers. She looked as if she had just crawled from bed: permed hair flattened into a sleep helmet; eyes swollen and glassy. When she spotted Carpo, she stopped in her tracks, blushing. One hand covered her mouth; the other tried to conceal the mess of hair.

"Sorry to bother you," Carpo said, hoping to put her at ease. "I'm here to speak to Trooper Walker."

Before the woman could speak, the trooper's voice floated in from the kitchen. "Go on, introduce yourself, Meg. It's the fellow I was telling you about. Jack Crawford's friend."

"Hi," the woman managed to get out, her hands still covering her mouth and hair.

Something about the woman's meekness and frailty, especially in relation to her husband's enormity, made Carpo feel sorry for her. "Don't worry," he whispered, "I'll only be a few minutes."

The woman nodded, then quietly backed from the room.

Trooper Walker returned with a mug in each hand. He gave one to Carpo, then motioned for them to be seated. Carpo settled on the couch; the plastic upholstery stuck to his exposed flesh like flypaper. Trooper Walker sat across from him.

"So what can I do for you, Michael?"

"I found something last night that I think you should know about."

Trooper Walker nodded, sipping coffee.

"I was cleaning the house and I came across a bowl of pork chops marinating in the refrigerator. Jack used to fix the same meal every time I visited. The chops have to marinate for eight hours, and he made them yesterday morning."

"And?"

"And there were enough pork chops for the two us."

Trooper Walker's eyes narrowed, but he didn't speak.

"What I'm trying to say is, Jack didn't commit suicide. He was murdered."

"Because of a bowl of pork chops, you think your friend was murdered?"

"I know it sounds wacky, but why would he go through the trouble of making them if he hadn't intended eating them?"

Trooper Walker set his cup down as if it were made of eggshell. "You sound like you've made up your mind about this."

"I have."

"Suicide's a strange thing, Michael. I don't know if you've ever been around it before, but people do some really odd things leading up to it. I've seen them fold their laundry, set the dinner table, even slip a roast in the oven before they stepped outside and blew their brains out. I'm inclined to stick with Doc Singer's ruling on this one. Jack Crawford slit his own two wrists."

Carpo wiggled forward on the couch. "Then what'd he do it with?"

"I suspect a razor or a knife."

"Where is it?"

The trooper shrugged. "Maybe he put it away."

"Where?" Carpo asked. "I cleaned that entire house yesterday. I didn't find a bloody knife or a bloody razor anywhere. I have a tough time believing that as Jack was dying he had the presence of mind to wipe off the knife and put it away."

"Amount of blood that spilled in that room, it wouldn't surprise me."

Carpo took a deep breath and reminded himself to be patient. "Let's say, for the sake of argument, he did wipe off and put away a knife. There are no knives in that bathroom, and the only razor blades are from shaving razors."

"Maybe he put it somewhere else."

"There would have been blood outside the bathroom."

"Maybe he cleaned it up."

Carpo closed his eyes and shook his head, showing the trooper that he needed to come up with a better explanation.

"Fine," Trooper Walker spat out, "if you've got all the answers, then answer this: If someone murdered Jack Crawford, why'd they do it the slowest way possible? Why not shoot him, or stab him, or slit his throat? And for that matter, why drag him into the bathroom to do it?"

"Obviously, so it would look like a suicide."

The trooper snapped his fingers. "But you're forgetting the dog, Michael, he was in the bathroom when it happened. If someone was attacking Jack Crawford, that mutt would have done something." He reached down and slapped the flanks of the dogs. "Hell, my boys would have shredded the person."

The dogs growled in unison, tails thumping against the floor.

Carpo considered whether he should try to describe

Floyd's temperament to the trooper. While Floyd may have looked big and intimidating, in reality he was a pussycat. He trusted all humans—even strangers—implicitly.

Trooper Walker stared at him, his face as blank and formidable as a brick wall. Suddenly, Carpo didn't feel like trying to get past it. "When does the morgue release the body?"

"Whenever they get instructions from the next of kin."

"And they're still going to skip an autopsy?"

"Like I told you, clear-cut suicides don't require them. And believe me, Michael, you may not like it, but this suicide was as clear-cut as they come."

Carpo didn't answer; there was nothing more to say. They both had their opinions, and Carpo had come to the wrong place to prove his. "Thank you for the coffee," he said abruptly, "I'm sorry to have disturbed you so early."

His legs made ripping sounds as they detached from the couch. As Trooper Walker steered him to the front door, his hand came to a rest on his shoulder. Carpo could feel the sweat leach through his shirt.

"Now, you just leave the police work to me," the trooper said. "I know you're upset about finding your friend like that. Who wouldn't be? But it's no reason to start going around town talking about murder. I don't need my job getting any busier with people thinking there's a killer on the loose." The trooper's hand lifted and then slapped Carpo's back with a resounding *thwack*.

"No problem," Carpo said, skin tingling from the slap.

Trooper Walker held the screen door for him. "Call if you need anything else."

Halfway out the door, Carpo stopped. "Actually, there

is something you can help with. I'm starting to get a lot of calls from the media, and just this morning a photographer parked in the driveway and started taking pictures of the cottage."

"Fucking press," Trooper Walker muttered, then, when he realized that Carpo was part of the press, added, "I can't do anything about the phone calls, but if anyone else drops by like that, call me. I'll post a squad car at the mouth of the driveway. That should keep things under control."

"That would be great."

It was the first time that morning they had agreed on something, and Trooper Walker grinned as if this fact made him happy. "Like I said, Michael, you just leave the police work to me. I'll take care of everything."

Five

After a quick stop at the market to buy his groceries for the week, Carpo returned to the cottage a little after one and spotted a yellow piece of paper fluttering from the front door. As he unlocked the door, he could see it was a handwritten message. Figuring it was from another reporter or photographer, he waited until he had carried in the groceries to read it.

To the young man tending Jack's place, the note stated in an elegant, flourished freehand, the kind taught years ago in penmanship classes. *I have just learned of Jack's untimely death. It is necessary for us to speak. I have information that could help you. Please visit this afternoon. I reside in the old Stewart homestead, above the Lillinonah marina. Regrets only—Elizabeth Jessup.*

Carpo put the note on the butcher block and fixed a pot of coffee. As he waited for the carafe to fill, he rolled the name Elizabeth Jessup around in his head. It sounded familiar, but he didn't know why. He wondered if Jack might have mentioned it in the past.

Since afternoon can mean anywhere from noon to six, Carpo split the difference; at three he climbed into his car and headed down Cooper Road, a steep, windy road that ended at a small marina on Lake Lillinonah. The old Stewart house overlooked the lake, a sprawling three-story home with a wraparound porch. Carpo had driven to the marina a few times over the years. He remembered that the house was accessible from a set of stairs in the marina parking lot.

A pair of sleek black Dobermans were at the top of the stairs as Carpo pulled into the gravel lot. As he rolled to a stop, the dogs charged the car, growling and nipping at the tires. The larger of the two—an enormous brute with a jaw so muscular, it looked deformed—put his paws on the driver-side window and bared his fangs two inches from Carpo's face. Luckily there was a piece of glass between them, which soon became flecked with the dog's hot breath.

An elderly black woman in a blue calico dress appeared at the top of the stairs. She had an odd bend to her body, weight tilted over a dented aluminum cane. As she stared down at Carpo, he was struck by her eyes—as gray and empty as fog. If he hadn't seen her walk to the steps, he would have figured she was completely blind.

The woman shouted something at the dogs. They made a high-pitched yelp as sharp as train brakes and retreated up the stairs. They stood at attention on either side of her, short tails quivering nervously. Carpo lowered his window a half-inch. "Ms. Jessup?" he called out. "It's Michael Carpo. You left a note at Jack's cottage."

"Yes, that's right," the woman said, the words tinged with a calypso lilt. "Come on up. These dogs, they won't bother you none."

Carpo opened the door, eyes on the dogs. They stayed fused to her legs, but their cropped ears were pitched forward in a menacing way. He wondered if it would be rude to carry a tire iron up to the house.

"Come, come, young man," the woman yelled, "be bold! They're all show, I promise it."

He ventured one foot out the door, then the other; the dogs remained at her side. Ignoring better instincts, he stepped out and closed the door.

The woman patted the big dog's head. "Silly young fellow, now, isn't he?"

As he started up the stairs, the big dog leaned over the edge and barked once. Carpo had begun to move toward the car when the woman yelled: "For Lord's sake, get up here! I am tired of waiting on you. I told you, my dogs won't hurt you none."

The ridicule in her voice was strong enough to overpower his feet. Checking back, he saw that both dogs were still at her side. He resumed his climb of the stairs. At the top the big dog greeted him with a gentle lick to the kneecap.

"I'm sorry," he said sheepishly. "I'm not used to Dobermans."

"All show, they're all show," the woman said, her face deforming into a prunish smile. She held out her hand. "I'm Bethie Jessup. I was Jack's next-door neighbor before we moved here to Bridgewater."

The woman's hand was so gnarled by arthritis, Carpo felt as if he was shaking a tree root. "Pleased to meet you," he said.

As they walked to the house, the dogs ran ahead of them and jumped into the shade beneath the wraparound porch. The house was enormous, and clearly old. The walls looked fortress thick, and supported a sagging wood-shingled roof.

A few of the windows still had the original hand-blown glass in them, the frosted panes providing a distorted image of the interior. The woman sat in a metal folding chair and waved Carpo into a bamboo cane chair. On the table between them rested a pitcher of iced tea with quartered lemons, clumps of ice, and a few sprigs of mint.

"Would you care for a cup of julep tea?" she offered.

"I'd love some."

As her crippled hand grasped the handle of the pitcher, Carpo made a motion to help, but the woman snapped: "Get away now, I can do it myself." And she did, pouring equal amounts of tea into two glasses without spilling.

She handed Carpo a glass and asked: "Now, what's your name again? Michael Car-pool?"

"No, it's Carpo. Michael Carpo."

"Let me see. Carpo. Carpo." She squinted fiercely, eyes vanishing in a skein of wrinkles. "There used to be a Tom Carpin over in Roxbury. Died back in the blizzard of 'forty-two. The fool froze to death walking his dog."

"We're not related."

"Of course not," she snorted. "You don't even have the same last name."

A breeze came off the lake, jingling metal chimes at the corner of the porch. Carpo sipped the iced tea. It was delicious—fresh brewed and sweetened with mint. Refreshing too.

The woman stared at the lake, lost in thought. Carpo wondered if she had forgotten him. He waited a minute, then said, "I hope I didn't come too early, Ms. Jessup."

"I said come this afternoon. It is afternoon."

She fell silent again, so Carpo tried a different tack. "I take it from your note that you know about Jack's death."

"Heard it on the radio this morning. Called the Litchfield County barracks straightaway, but they'd only confirm that he died." Her eyes left the lake and came to rest on Carpo. "I was hoping you'd fill in the missing parts."

"I found his body," he said, deciding at that moment to tell what he believed about Jack. "The police have ruled it a suicide, but I don't think it was."

"No," she whispered, head bobbing up and down in a yes motion, "I wouldn't think so."

"I think he was murdered," Carpo added.

"Yes," she said, head moving side to side in a no motion, "just like all the rest."

The woman's answers and contradictory head motions confused Carpo. He set his glass on the table. "What are you saying, Ms. Jessup? Have there been other deaths in town?"

"For two, maybe three years now. Answer me something, son. How did you find Jack?"

"His wrists were slit. As if he'd committed suicide."

"I heard that from the radio. What I want to know is where you found him."

"In the bathroom."

"Now tell me about the door. Was it shut tight?"

Carpo recalled his discovery of Jack's body. "Yes, it was closed."

"And I'll bet that damn fool dog of his, Fran, or whatever his name is, I'll bet he was in there too."

Carpo's skin tingled. "How do you know all this?"

"And the front door. Was that open too?"

"Ms. Jessup, were you in the cottage after Jack died?"

The woman stared again at the lake, then quietly asked, "Son, have you ever heard of a thing called a ripple?"

"As in a water ripple?"

"In a way, it is like that." She took a deep breath and held it, as if steeling herself for a difficult task. Then she said, "When a person enters this world, they cross a threshold from the beyond to the here. That threshold stays open for them, sometimes one hundred years, sometimes more, waiting for the person to exit again. But some of us leave before it was intended. Accident. Murder. Suicide. They leave, but the threshold stays open. It waits and waits and waits. That's what's known as a ripple."

He wanted to ask how this pertained to Jack, but the woman beat him to a question. "Tell me something about Jack's dog," she said. "Is he acting all skittish around that bathroom? Like he's scared to go in there?"

He remembered how Floyd had acted outside the bathroom yesterday, yelping in terror when he petted him. "I guess he's a little nervous. He doesn't seem to want to go in there."

"That's because he can sense it. He can sense the ripple. Now, listen to me good. I suggest you be mightily careful in that cottage. This ripple is nothing to fool with. I warned Jack about a similar thing two years ago. He just laughed at me. Now he's gone and created one himself."

"But I still don't understand. Is this ripple like a haunted spot? Like Jack's haunting the cottage?"

The woman waved a hand with contempt. "That's plum silly, son. I surely don't believe in ghosts, if that's what you're implying. It's like this. A ripple happens when a person doesn't leave the world as it was intended. That's why Jack's dog is staying out of that bathroom. Animals can feel the ripple, and it frightens them."

"Then there must be millions of these ripples," Carpo said. "Just think of New York City. Hundreds of people get murdered there every year."

"And that's why I'll never visit that city. There's thousands and thousands of ripples there, in just about every building." She scratched her chin like an ancient sage. "That's why so many crazies end up in the big cities. They can sense the ripples just like dogs can, only they're not scared of them, they're attracted to them."

Carpo wondered what type of person Elizabeth Jessup would label as crazy; the whole ripple theory sounded utterly insane. About the only reason he didn't scoff openly at her theory was the accurate description she had provided of the way he found Jack's body. "Is this ripple thing how you know so much about the cottage?" he asked.

"Let me tell you a quick story, maybe you'll understand better. Fifty years ago, me and Jack was next-door neighbors in a little town nestled in the Housatonic valley. We lived near an old woman named Evelyn Baird. Miss Baird was a saintly person; she hated to see things suffer. If there was a bird with a broken wing, she'd take it in her house and nurse it to health. She also looked after the stray cats in town. Must have been a dozen lived in that house, climbing over the furniture, digging up the flowers, I'll never know how she stood for it.

"One Sunday my mama noticed Miss Baird hadn't made it to church, so she sent my daddy to check on her. They found Miss Baird in the bathroom with all the animals—

cats and birds—stuck in there. She'd been murdered, her throat slit from ear to ear. The police said it was a robbery, which we all thought strange because nothing was missing.

"Few nights later I heard my parents talking about Miss Baird's house and whether there was a ripple in it. That's the first I heard that term. They planned to take my little dog, Scat, over to see if he was afraid of that bathroom. They never got a chance. In the middle of the night someone set the house on fire. Jack and I rode our bikes over and watched it burn. What a fire it was. All of Miss Baird's cats was still inside, and they were screaming like the devil himself. A whole chorus of devils. That night the smell of singed fur sat over that town."

The woman looked over the lake, her voice now as weak as a whisper. "And that's when things started going bad in town. I think maybe Miss Baird and them cats opened up a whole big ripple in that town. After that things went bad for all of us. Real bad."

"And you think this is somehow related to Jack's death?"

The woman put both hands on the cane and shifted her weight. "I don't know," she said. "The way Jack's body was found, it sure does sound similar to what I saw as a girl. Maybe there's others who remember Evelyn Baird besides me."

Though he wasn't sure if he believed the woman, her story sent a shiver through him. He picked up his glass and drained the last drop of the iced tea.

"Can I pour you more?" she offered.

"No, thanks, Ms. Jessup. In fact, I should probably be getting back. Was there anything else you wanted to tell me?"

"That's all. I wanted to warn you to be careful, because it'll happen again. Sure as I'm sitting here, this killing is not finished."

"You'd better be careful yourself."

The woman's face broke into a smile so wrinkled it could have cracked a Teflon pan. "I'm not stubborn like Jack," she said. "I have two dogs to watch out for me, and they watch well. If that fails, I can always fall back on this."

The woman lifted her dress above her knee, revealing a swollen, disfigured leg. Carpo watched in horror as she moved the dress higher, past her hip, to the top of her dark green panty hose. There, tucked in the elastic waistband, was a derringer. She plucked out the tiny black gun, waving it for emphasis. "This will keep me safe," she cackled. "This will keep my ripple from forming."

Elizabeth Jessup isn't crazy, Carpo decided. *She's certifiably insane.*

She thrust the gun back in her hose and dropped the dress, concealing the weapon. Then she used her cane to push out of the metal chair. As soon as the dogs heard the chair creak, they raced to her side. Carpo guessed they had been under the floor, watching through the cracks in the boards. When she moved, they moved.

Carpo followed her down the path to the parking lot, noting how the dogs strayed no more than a nose length behind or in front of her. They did more than watch her; they stayed glued to her sides. Which brought another question to mind. When they reached the stairs, he asked, "Ms. Jessup, do you own a car?"

"I've got enough trouble seeing the tip of this cane. How would I see the road?"

"Then I was wondering how you dropped off that note at the cottage this afternoon."

"A friend was by this morning. They delivered it for me."

Carpo shook the old woman's hand and said good-bye. Then he reached down and patted the head of the big dog, just to remind him that he was a friend. He walked down the stairs. Before getting in his car he thought of one other question. "Ms. Jessup, what was the name of that town you and Jack lived in?"

"Southville."

"Was it near here?"

"No more than a stone's throw." The woman broke into a cackle again, then she tipped an imaginary hat. "Good afternoon, young man. And remember my warning."

As Carpo opened the car door, he saw a shiny black blur move down the stairs. He jumped in the car and slammed the door just as the big dog's snout collided with the window. The dog stayed pinned to the door—teeth bared, spittle flying—until Carpo pulled out of the marina.

Six

The meeting with Elizabeth Jessup had created more questions than answers in Carpo's mind. What did a murder in another town fifty years ago have to do with Jack's death? And how much weight should he give to her wacky theories on thresholds, ripples, and untimely deaths? Common sense told him to discard the entire conversation. Instead, when he returned to the cottage, he decided to conduct a simple experiment.

He walked into the living room and whistled for Floyd, who emerged from the bedroom, groggy from his nap. Then Carpo stepped into the bathroom and called for Floyd to follow. The dog inched forward, neck outstretched, nose sniffing the ground, but when he reached the threshold of the bathroom, he stopped.

"Come on, Floyd," Carpo coaxed. "Come here."

The dog whined faintly but did not move.

Carpo cursed, then quickly settled on a different approach. *If I can't overcome his mind,* he thought, *I'll conquer his belly.* He walked into the kitchen and grabbed a handful of dog biscuits; the rattle of the jar top brought Floyd racing in. Carpo showed him the biscuits, then led him back to the living room. He dangled a treat before the dog's nose, a long, tempting whiff; the dog's salivary glands roared to life, drool spilling from his mouth. Then Carpo stepped into the bathroom and put the treat on the floor.

Floyd edged forward, licking his lips, but still did not enter.

Carpo coaxed him. Tossed him treats. Even formed a row of them across the floor, starting in the living room, to see if the dog might unwittingly enter the room. Each time the result was the same: Floyd greedily munched the treats he could reach, but when his nose touched the threshold he halted, as if an invisible hand had tugged him back.

"Dammit, Floyd! Get in here!"

It was ludicrous. Completely ridiculous. A batty old woman had freaked Carpo out, and now he needed Floyd to prove her wrong.

"Heel!" he ordered the dog. "Heel!"

Floyd whined and pawed the floor, but that was as close as he came to touching the white tile. *This is crazy,* Carpo thought. *This entire thing is insane. Ripples, doorways, and cursed towns.*

He tried to rationalize Floyd's behavior. Perhaps a trace of Jack's blood lingered in the tile grout. Or maybe the dog still associated the bathroom with the place where his master had died. Whatever the reason, Carpo's temper got the best of him. He leapt at the dog and snared him by the neck. With one hand clamped on the loose flesh there, the other snagged the dog's tail. Then, with one quick motion, he tossed Floyd into the bathroom.

He might as well have just beaten the dog.

Floyd yelped hysterically, as if pinned to an electric fence. He wiggled free of Carpo's grip and fled to the living room, darting into the shadows beneath Jack's desk. When Carpo heard the dog's pathetic whimpers, his heart plummeted. He returned to the kitchen for another handful of treats. Then he got on his hands and knees and crawled into the dark space. He fed the biscuits to Floyd, one at a time, until he eventually coaxed the dog from the darkness.

Whether or not Elizabeth Jessup was crazy seemed terribly unimportant now. What he had done to Floyd was wrong. Carpo swore to himself that no matter what, he would never force Floyd to enter the bathroom again.

Seven

Carpo finally got through to Jack's sister, Kyra, in Athens, Georgia. For the amount of time he'd been dreading the call, it turned out to be a relatively painless conversation. A reporter from *The New York Times* had contacted her early that morning, so she'd had almost the entire day to digest the bad news. Carpo relayed his sympathies to the family and pledged to help them settle Jack's affairs in Bridgewater.

Kyra announced that Jack's remains would be shipped to Athens and buried in the family plot. She also said that the family planned to sell Jack's cottage, and she asked Carpo to find someone to take in Floyd. Carpo decided that it would not be prudent to mention his theory about Jack's death. At least, not yet.

When he got off the phone, it was seven-thirty; the sun was on a dramatic collision course with the far side of the valley. He sauntered into the kitchen and poured a whiskey, then took it to the patio, pulling around one of the wooden Adirondack chairs so he could face the lake. Nature and the whiskey did a fine job of relaxing him. A pair of squirrels bounced around the lawn, gathering acorns, and a wild canary flew into the bird feeder for some seed. High over the valley, a hawk hovered with its wings set, motionless, as if suspended by an invisible string.

An amazing amount of wildlife thrived in that corner of Connecticut, some of it in numbers greater than when Native Americans were the only residents. Over the years on Jack's seventeen acres of land, Carpo had spotted deer, raccoon, possum, fox, and coyote. The bird population was equally diverse: pheasants, woodpeckers, mourning doves, hummingbirds, blue jays, cardinals, and even turkeys.

Fresh air, privacy, and open space: It was no mystery why he felt so comfortable there. In New York he existed in a cramped one-bedroom apartment in the East Village, where the silence was disrupted once an hour by fire and police sirens or car alarms. It happened so frequently, he didn't even notice them anymore. Contrast that with Bridgewater, where the only noises after dark were cricket chirps and frog croaks. Never in his life had Carpo heard a more deafening silence.

After he finished the whiskey, he went to the kitchen to make dinner. He decided on chicken cutlets sautéed in butter, shallots, and white wine. Not exactly healthful in this day of low-fat, low-cholesterol, low-taste cooking, but nothing set his mouth watering faster than the smell of shallots sautéing in melted butter.

As the chicken browned, Carpo quickly shucked three ears of local sweet corn and tossed them into a pot of boiling water. He also picked two mutant-sized tomatoes from the garden, sliced them into wedges, and poured olive oil over them. When the chicken was done, he uncorked a bottle of red wine and carried the feast to the porch. Floyd was his only dinner companion; Carpo rewarded him with scraps of leftover chicken skin.

By the time he had rinsed and filed the dishes into the dishwasher, he was exhausted. He didn't even bother to check if the doors were locked before heading to bed. Seconds after laying down his head, he was sound asleep.

Sometime during the night the sound of a siren awakened him. It wasn't loud—nothing like the window-rattling sirens in New York City—and perhaps that was why it awakened him. At first he thought it was the town's fire alarm. The local brigade called its members with a loud horn that could be heard all the way at the cottage. But this siren was different; it was moving. Up Beach Hill Road, past the cottage, then down Skyline Ridge toward the marina. After twenty or thirty seconds it faded away. Carpo was cognizant enough to check the clock—five forty-three—before he fell back asleep.

Two hours later the sound of Amanda's clippers in the garden awakened him. He put a pot of coffee on, then went to the bathroom and splashed cold water on his face. He dragged a wet comb across his head, turning his hair as dark and shiny as motor oil. He filled two mugs with coffee, then walked out to the garden.

Amanda was wading through a shoulder-high patch of sunflowers. The large round flowers were heavy with black seeds, causing the stems to droop; they leaned toward her in unison, like an audience of yellow Cyclops. Carpo understood their attraction. Dressed in a gray T-shirt, faded khaki shorts, with a blue checkered scarf knotted at her neck, Amanda epitomized the concept of simple beauty.

But as he drew closer, he noticed that something was wrong with her. Her face was drawn, eyes tired and dull. After they said good morning and he handed her a mug, he asked: "You okay, Amanda?"

The steam from the coffee shimmered past her eyes like mist on a cold blue ocean. In a whisper she said, "I barely slept last night."

"What happened?"

"There was an accident down at the marina."

He nodded, remembering what woke him up in the middle the night. "I heard the siren come up Beach Hill last night. Who got hurt?"

"The old woman who lives down there."

"Do you mean Elizabeth Jessup?"

"Yes, Bethie Jessup." Amanda frowned. "Did you know her?"

"We met yesterday. She left a note tacked to the door, asking me to visit. What did the police say? Was it an accident?"

Amanda ignored his question. "I put that letter on your door. What did she say to you?"

"She wanted to discuss Jack's death."

Amanda set her coffee on the fence post. Then she took the garden shears out of her pocket and started clipping sunflowers. The air smelled like fresh sap. "What did she say about Jack?" she asked without looking up.

Something about the question felt odd to Carpo, the way she had asked it. Coolly, as if his answer didn't really matter, even though she had repeated it twice. On an impulse he decided to lie. "She asked what was going to happen to Floyd after I leave. She said she wanted to adopt him."

Amanda straightened, frowning. "Bethie wanted to adopt Floyd? You've got to be kidding. She hated him."

As soon as she said it, Carpo remembered how the old woman had referred to Floyd as a *damn fool dog.* He could have kicked himself for forgetting. "That's what she said," he insisted. "She wanted to take him in until I could find a proper home for him. Personally, I think she was trying to see if I would take him."

"Did she say anything else?"

"No, we talked for only a few minutes." Carpo sipped his coffee; he needed to change the subject. "So what happened to her?"

"She drowned in the lake."

"How did you hear about it?"

"I was the one who found her."

"Oh, God," Carpo gasped. "What happened?"

"Late last night I heard her dogs barking. I called her house, but there was no answer. Finally, I went down there to see what was wrong."

"Where was she?"

"Next to the dock. Floating in about three feet of water."

"Any idea what happened?"

"The local trooper thinks she slipped and hit her head."

"Do you think so too?"

"It's possible," she said, shrugging, "but it doesn't explain why she was on the dock in the first place. She knew that place like the back of her hand. I can't imagine why she'd walk down to the dock in the middle of the night."

"How long did you know her?"

Amanda gathered the cut sunflowers. "Bethie and I got close about two years ago. I was working on a painting about a piece of local folklore. She had some information on it, so I interviewed her. We hit it off, and kept in touch ever since."

"She seemed a bit . . . eccentric to me."

"If you didn't know her, you might think that. She had her foibles, but Bethie was just a nice old lady. Nicer than just about anyone else in this town." Amanda shook her head. "I'm going to miss her, Michael. I'm really going to miss her."

Carpo had serious doubts that Elizabeth Jessup's death was an accident, but he kept his opinion to himself around Amanda. That's because he was starting to have serious doubts about Amanda.

When he got past her stunning looks and disarming smile, he really didn't know much about the woman. And then there was the strange fact that Jack had never mentioned her before. It seemed like every summer Jack would try to set him up with someone—this friend's daughter or that neighbor's houseguest. Not once had Amanda Cutler's name come up. She had lived up the road for two years, and by her account had been close friends with Jack, but for some unknown reason he had forgotten to tell Carpo about the beautiful young painter who stopped by his cottage every morning to clip his prized flowers.

One thing bothered Carpo: timing. Two deaths in less than three days, and Amanda had been on the scene for both. She was the last person to see Jack alive Sunday morning and the first person to spot Elizabeth Jessup floating in Lake Lillinonah Monday night. He had a tough time believing that it was all due to bad luck.

It was time to pay another visit to Trooper Walker, to see if Elizabeth Jessup's death had changed his opinion about Jack's suicide, but first he needed some ammunition. There was a sign taped to the wall in the Channel 8 newsroom: *Know the answer before you ask the question.* Carpo wanted to have some facts when he confronted Trooper Walker, and he believed the best place to find them was the New Milford Public Library.

New Milford was a fifteen-minute drive from the cottage; it was a larger town than Bridgewater, famous for its pristine town green, a quarter-mile strip of grass with a gazebo and a small World War I army tank parked at one end. The library was in the middle of the green, between a stone church and an old colonial home.

Even though Carpo didn't know what he was looking for, his instincts told him to start at a library; being a journalist, he already understood the resources that a library provided. Often, the best libraries were the smallest ones. They tended to have better primary sources: clippings from local newspapers, historical papers, census documents, and tax information. They also provided a less tangible yet just as valuable form of resource: local gossip.

Carpo found just such a resource sitting at the reference desk—a tiny woman with a mountain of snow-white hair and large horn-rimmed glasses. The sign on the desk identified her: *Dorothy Elwes, Research Librarian.*

Carpo introduced himself as an employee of Channel 8 News; he figured it would raise fewer questions about why he was digging for information. He told the woman that he was interested in gathering some facts about the neighboring town of Bridgewater.

Dorothy had a habit of pursing her lips together in quick spasms just before speaking, as if she wanted to whistle but couldn't settle on the proper tune. "Have you tried the Burnham Library?" she asked, referring to the local library in Bridgewater. "If you want information on Bridgewater, that's the place to start."

"Yes, but it's closed," Carpo said, his answer only partly true. The library was closed, but even if it had been open he wouldn't have gone there. Gossip worked in both directions; he didn't want to risk word leaking out that he was doing research on the town.

"Well, I can certainly accommodate you here," she said happily. "Bridgewater was once part of New Milford, so we have excellent archives on its incorporation as a separate town."

"How long ago was that?"

"The incorporation—1856. Before that Bridgewater was called Sheep's Neck, because of its shape." Dorothy's lips twitched a few times. "What period are you interested in, dear?"

"Nothing that far back. A famous writer died in Bridgewater this past Sunday. I'm planning an obituary for one of our shows and I thought it might be interesting to do a sidebar on Bridgewater. Something to add a little local flavor."

"Terrible news, just terrible," she said in reference to Jack. "I suggest we start with back editions of *The New Milford Times*, our local paper, which covers Bridgewater and a few other towns in the county."

She led Carpo to a wall of filing cabinets in the back of the library and told him that it was filled with microfilm cassettes of the newspaper going all the way back to the 1800s. She also showed him a rack of reference books that contained chapters on the history of Bridgewater. Finally, she showed him a file containing research papers and various government reports dealing with the town's incorporation.

Before he knew it, Carpo had a stack of materials that would have taken a week to sort through. Since he didn't have that kind of time, he decided to begin with *The New Milford Times*. Dorothy offered him a locked study room for privacy and the use of his own microfilm machine. Carpo gathered the issues from the past five years, arranged them on the room's bare metal desk, and set to work.

He started by speed-reading the front pages of the newspapers and jotting down quick notes on articles or stories about Bridgewater that seemed unusual or interesting. Many articles chronicled the comings, goings, and doings of Bridgewater's first selectman, Billy Stubbs, the town's highest elected official. Other stories centered on fiscal issues: taxes for the local school, road repairs, a new roof for the town hall, and the purchase of a new snowplow for the town garage. The photographs and articles chronicled a strange mix of life and death in this small country town: a pictorial on the application of a fresh coat of silver paint on the Lillinonah bridge; a story on Arnie Scofield, the first Bridgewater boy in forty-three years to make eagle scout, and a snapshot of the wreckage left by Clifford Hughes's car the night he plowed into an oak tree on Route 133.

It took a while for a pattern to develop, but Carpo soon noticed the nasty streak of accidents and deaths occurring in Bridgewater. When he reached the end of the papers, he reread them. This time he took copious notes on any story dealing with an unusual or unnatural death. Going back two years, he found six such stories. And that didn't count the two deaths that had occurred since his arrival on Sunday.

It started October 3, 1996, with the death of sixty-two-year-old Karla Phelan in the Pratt Nature Preserve, along the shores of Lake Lillinonah. That morning Karla had packed a knapsack with a small lunch, her watercolors, and a portable easel, intending to spend a few hours painting and hiking in the woods. When she didn't return by dinner-time, her family called the police. The next morning a group of schoolchildren walking to the bus spotted her body in the lake. The Litchfield County coroner—Doc Singer himself—ruled the death an accidental drowning. Noting the uneven contusion at the back of her head, Singer surmised that the woman had slipped in the shallows and hit her head on a rock.

Carpo made a note in the margin: *Check location E.J.'s contusion.*

On December 22 of the same year, seventy-year-old Claudell Jenkins committed suicide by jumping off the Lilli-nonah bridge. Bridgewater's state trooper—Trooper Walker himself—spotted a bundle of neatly folded clothes and red Reeboks halfway across the pedestrian walkway. He also discovered a short, typed note by the victim saying that he had been diagnosed with an aggressive form of bone cancer.

One week later, sixty-seven-year-old Charlie Simms electrocuted himself in his home. His daughter found the body. Doc Singer ruled the death an accident, saying the man's finger had come in contact with an open socket while changing a lightbulb. A jolt of electricity had passed through the man, nonfatal to most people, except Charlie Simms suffered from a chronic heart condition.

Bridgewater was quiet until May 17, 1997, when Clifford Hughes had his car accident. A brief obituary sat alongside the photograph of the red pickup truck smashed against the oak tree. Despite the grainy quality of the photo, snapped at night, it was possible to see Mr. Hughes's mangled body protruding from the cab's rear window.

In the margin Carpo scribbled: *Front vs. rear.*

Six months later, Charlotte Thigpen, age eighty-two, died of a broken neck after falling down the stairs. Carpo knew that accidental falls were a leading cause of death among the elderly, but two things in the story caught his attention. Charlotte had been home alone at the time of the accident, and her son said that he had warned Charlotte a week earlier not to use the basement stairs anymore.

So he jotted: *Alone. Warned.*

Another stretch of calm descended on Bridgewater that lasted through the winter and spring of 1998. On June 14, two months to the day before Carpo discovered Jack's body, Frank Washington, age seventy-one, died from an allergic reaction to beestings. He had been mowing the lawn, when the wheel of his tractor struck a hornet's nest. He died before he could make it inside the house. The death seemed too spontaneous to be anything but an accident, but then Carpo read that Trooper Walker had found Frank Washington's dog, Tripper, locked in the bathroom.

Tripper. Floyd. Bathroom.

He had his ammunition. Now it was time to use it on Trooper Walker.

* * *

Trooper Walker did not look happy when he answered the door at his house. His eyebrows crinkled together, one ridge higher than the other, his eyes as dark and foreboding as a double-barreled shotgun. "What is it now?" the trooper asked. "The press still bothering you?"

In one hand Carpo held a piece of paper with the names he had culled from *The New Milford Times*, in the other, photocopies of the articles to back up the list.

"See this?" He waved the list of names. "These are the names of eight people who have died in Bridgewater from unnatural causes in the past two years, including Jack Crawford and Elizabeth Jessup. Now, are you going to keep on claiming that there's nothing wrong in town?"

The screen door cast a tiny square-shaped pattern on the trooper's face that seemed to chart the distance between his gaping mouth and his unblinking eyes. "For Christ's sake, are you still hung up on this thing? Jack Crawford slit his own two wrists, and it has nothing to do with any other death in town. Do me a favor, Michael, go back to New York City. It's time for you to go home."

Trooper Walker gave a half-nod, then stepped back from the screen and started to shut the door.

"If you shut that door, I will go back to the city. I'll take this story to my television station and I'll do a story on it. Channel 8 reaches up here, and I'm sure every newspaper in the state will pick up on it."

The door stopped moving. "You threatening me?" Trooper Walker asked icily.

"All I'm saying is you can deal with it now or when it hits the airwaves. I think a lot of people will want to know why you've ignored so many deaths." Carpo put his hand on the screen door. "May I come in and show you what I found?"

The trooper stood immobile. Then he stepped aside so Carpo could enter. They walked back to the same room as before. Carpo took his spot on the couch. Trooper Walker squeezed into his chair. This time there were no offers of coffee. Trooper Walker stared at the piece of paper in Carpo's hands, as if trying to gauge its contents. Finally, he motioned for it.

He studied the list for several minutes, his throat making odd sounds as he read the names. Noises like *hmph*, or *a-hmph*. Suddenly, he pointed at Clifford Hughes's name.

"I was the first on the scene that night," he stated confidently. "Not a damn thing unusual about a car wreck, especially on Route 133. Cliff's wheel went into the gully, and he couldn't pull back before the tree."

"The truck was pushed into the tree."

"Hell it was. I investigated that crash. It was an accident."

Carpo had been prepared for the trooper to challenge his assertions. He pulled the photograph of the car wreck from his bundle of clippings. "Look at the dent in the rear bumper and look at the body. How many frontal impacts have you seen where the person flies out the back window? His car was struck from behind."

The trooper glared at the photograph. He opened his mouth, but no sound came out. Carpo had him, and there was no arguing.

"Karla Phelan," the trooper said, pointing at the woman who drowned in Lake Lillinonah. "How's that a murder?"

Carpo shuffled to the corresponding article in his pile. "It says here, the schoolchildren who found her body said she was floating facedown. And in Doc Singer's report he said that he found a contusion at the back of her head. How many people fall backward and hit their head, then flip face forward and drown?"

"I can think of a million ways, none malicious."

"Name one."

"Maybe the tide flipped her over, or the wake from a powerboat, or even the wind." The trooper smirked. "That's three right there."

"Just out of curiosity, did Elizabeth Jessup have a contusion on her head too?"

The trooper didn't say anything.

"I'll bet it was on the back of her head," Carpo continued, "and I'll also bet she was found facedown."

The trooper looked back at the list, muttering under his breath. Carpo figured that meant the answer to Elizabeth Jessup was the same as Karla Phelan: hit on the back, drowned on the front.

"Frank Washington," the trooper snorted. "Frank died of beestings. More than forty of them. Now, I suppose you're going to sit there and tell me that someone planted a beehive in his yard and then did something to the tractor tire to make sure it ran over it. Bullshit. I don't care what you pull out of that pile of clippings there, this was an accident."

"I don't have an answer for that one yet."

"I knew it," the trooper exclaimed triumphantly. "See, you can't be waving this list in front of me like it's hard evidence, because it isn't. Take Charlotte Thigpen. Old people fall down the stairs every day. Or Claudell Jenkins. The man left a signed suicide note. How much more proof do you need?"

"I'll admit, some of these are shaky. But you've got to admit that there's a lot of people dying in town. You should start taking it seriously."

The trooper's face turned red. "You've got a hell of a nerve coming in my house and accusing me of that."

"I'm not accusing you of anything, Trooper Walker. All I'm saying is that people are dying, and they're not all accidents. You can either start taking it seriously or . . ." Carpo allowed his voice to trail off ominously.

"Or what? You'll run to your big-shot TV station and do a story on me? I won't be threatened by you, Carpo. No one is above the law, and that includes you."

"I'm not threatening you. If you really have been doing your job, you have nothing to worry about."

The trooper began pacing the room, fuming. "Unreal. Un-fucking-real," he said. "Do you know what'll happen if you run a story on this? I'll have senior citizen groups crawling over this town like a bunch of roaches. Go ahead, nod your head all you like, but think for a second what it'll do to Bridgewater."

He continued nodding to show that he had considered what such a story would do to the town, and that he would run it anyway.

Carpo didn't stay long at the trooper's house; he had accomplished everything he had set out to do. First, he had gotten the point across to Trooper Walker that Jack Crawford's death needed to be reopened. Second, and more important, he had proven to himself that Trooper Walker knew how the deaths were linked. All eight of them.

The deaths had one common fact, one unique characteristic, that proved something more was happening in Bridgewater than a random series of accidents and suicides. Carpo knew it. Trooper Walker knew it. Probably every person in town knew it.

He had given the trooper a slip of paper with eight names written on it: Jack Crawford, Elizabeth Jessup, Claudell Jenkins, Karla Phelan, Charlie Simms, Frank Washington, Clifford Hughes, and Charlotte Thigpen. Eight names, nothing else. No newspaper articles, no photographs, no descriptions of the victims. Yet Trooper Walker had recalled enough about each person to mention senior citizen groups. That was because Trooper Walker knew exactly what Carpo had discovered at the New Milford Public Library. The common link between the eight victims was their age. Every person who had died was over the age of sixty-five.

Eight

Floyd nearly leapt into Carpo's arms when he got back to the cottage, the dog was so happy to see him. It was a nice greeting, the kind of welcome that didn't make it so hard to return to an empty house.

Or maybe, Carpo thought, *an empty apartment.*

Floyd had been on his mind ever since he had promised Jack's sister that he would find a home for the dog. He had four days left in the country, which meant that he had four days to decide Floyd's future. Where would he find a home for him?

He poured a glass of orange juice and carried it into the living room, taking a seat on the couch. Floyd stood before him, wet nose nudging his hand. When he didn't respond fast enough, the dog plopped an enormous paw on his knee, nails curling into his skin like cat claws. He patted the dog on the head, then scratched behind each ear. Floyd's body grew rigid, and he leaned into every spot that Carpo scratched, as if to maximize the intensity of the contact point. Slowly, Carpo scratched down his neck and across his spine until he was rubbing the fur between his hindquarters. The result was instant doggie Shangri-la; Floyd's whole body stiffened and he rocked back and forth in spasmodic response to the scratching.

"You like that, don't you, boy?"

Floyd responded with a lazy turn of the head, lower lip curled ecstatically as his butt continued its strange gyrations.

The dog's fur was full of natural oils; Carpo's hands felt as if they had moisturizer on them. They smelled good too: maple syrup mixed with dirt and leaves, like the woods in late fall.

But how will Floyd smell in filthy New York?

Carpo considered every reason that he should not bring Floyd to the city. His apartment was cramped, and Floyd would be alone ten or more hours while he was at work. Furthermore, Manhattan was no place for a breed like a Labrador: large dogs that need to roam free in the woods, chasing birds and squirrels. The nicest park near Twelfth Street was Gramercy Park, eight blocks to the north and one avenue to the west. It was a beautiful, clean, safe park. Unfortunately, it was also a private park; Carpo knew that he didn't have a chance of convincing the powers that be to give him a key to the gate.

But it was either bring Floyd to New York or never see him again. The second possibility did not sit well with Carpo. Nor with Floyd, who wedged his nose under Carpo's wrist and flipped it into the air, catapulting his hand onto his back. Carpo resumed scratching.

"That's a good boy, Floyd. You're a good dog."

Carpo drained his orange juice and returned to the kitchen to fix lunch. He toasted an onion bagel and stacked it with salami, Swiss cheese, and a generous amount of Dijon mustard. Then he refilled his glass with seltzer water and returned to the living room. Floyd followed again, this time his attention focused on what Carpo was holding. The sight of the sandwich, with its scent of meat and cheese, caused him to drool.

"Knock it off, Floyd." Carpo pushed him away with his foot; the dog slumped to the floor, a dejected groan rumbling in his throat. "I hear you, but if you're planning to move to New York with me, this drooling thing has got to stop."

There, he had said it. And without quite realizing it, he had made up his mind. Somehow, some way, Floyd would be making the trip home with him.

As he tore into the sandwich, his thoughts shifted to the rest of Jack's belongings. Jack's sister had said that she planned to sell the cottage and all of its contents, and she asked Carpo if there was anything he would like to take for himself. There was so much that interested him, he didn't know where to start. First, there were the photographs. Dozens of black-and-whites hanging on the walls in simple lacquered-wood frames. His favorite was the shot on the mantel of Jack in his navy uniform just before he sailed for the Pacific. He also liked the wedding photo of Jack and Effie marching down the aisle of Abyssinian Baptist Church in Harlem. There were also shots of Jack alongside various creative giants of the century. Dinner in Paris with Ralph Ellison. Drinks in Key West with Tennessee Williams. A backstage meeting with Maria Callas at the old Metropolitan Opera House. Then there was the publicity photograph that Irving Penn had taken, a moody, evocative portrait that showed Jack behind his Smith Corona, a gray fedora poised on his head and a black cigar fuming in the ashtray at his elbow.

Besides the photographs, there were Jack's letters to consider. Thousands of them, stored in five cardboard boxes in the basement. Carpo figured he could spend the rest of his life wading through all the postcards, letters, and correspondence that Jack had kept with so many literary luminaries: Tennessee Williams, William Faulkner, Zora Neale Hurston, Robert Penn Warren, Carson McCullers, Arthur Miller, Ralph Ellison, Richard Wright, and James Baldwin. The letters fascinated Carpo because they covered such diverse writers: Communist to conservative, beatnik to formalist, theorist to novelist. Only Jack could have united so many opposites.

The most formidable of Jack's possessions were his books. Hundreds of them, perhaps thousands, lined not only the three walls of the living room but two walls in each bedroom. The shelves ran floor to ceiling, creating blocks of color and text as decorative as the tiles of a mosaic or the stitches in a tapestry. Jack once claimed that he had read every book in the cottage at least once. At first Carpo had doubted this claim, mainly because of the sheer number of books on the shelves; in the time since, he had grown to believe it.

"Every man has a fetish," Jack had announced one night when he caught Carpo staring at the shelves. "Mine is books. I can't resist them. Buying them, holding them, reading them. I can't even resist their smell."

Carpo must have had a skeptical look on his face, because Jack reached over his head and plucked a worn, leather-bound volume of Ovid's *Metamorphoses* off the shelf. He blew across its top, spraying fine dust in the air, then handed the book to Carpo.

"Feel that. Doesn't it just fit perfectly in your hand? It's like a baseball mitt, the leather so soft and worn, so perfectly balanced. And try this." Jack opened the book and held the pages under his nose. "Smell it. Go on, take a whiff."

Reluctantly, Carpo closed his eyes and inhaled. His head jerked up, nostrils tickled by the peppery odor emanating from the pages, a dusty smell with an essence of the ancient wood from which the pages had been shaved.

"Doesn't it smell wonderful, Carpo? Remember it, it's the odor of greatness, of real achievement. And every single one of these books has its own distinct aroma."

With his nose still pressed to the book, Carpo noticed several bits of paper poking from the pages. Jack noticed them too.

"Those are my memory markers," he explained, taking the book back and flipping through the pages. "Every time I come across a passage that inspires me or teaches me something, I slip a marker in there so I can find it again."

"Let me see."

"No, wait, I've got a good one for you." Jack replaced Ovid to the shelf, moved down two shelves, and removed a thicker book: *How to Win Friends and Influence People* by Dale Carnegie. Carpo blushed, wondering if Jack was insinuating that he needed help in the interpersonal relations department.

Jack saw his face and chuckled. "Relax, Carpo, let me explain. There was a time not so long ago—definitely not long enough ago—when they used to ban books in this country. Now, I'm not talking about some hillbilly school district that outlaws *Catcher in the Rye* as gay porn, I mean a ban where the book can't be found anywhere in the country. The writer of this book had one of his most famous works banned for years."

Carpo was puzzled by what Jack was saying, especially since he had never heard of Dale Carnegie having trouble with the censors, but when he opened the book, he instantly understood. Within the recognizable cover was a second text: *Sexus* by Henry Miller.

"I snuck that into the country in 1962," Jack recalled fondly. "Felt like a subversive, a smuggler of contraband. Now, that wasn't the book that was banned, it happened with another title of Miller's a few years earlier, but even after the ban was lifted you couldn't find his work in many places. I bought that copy in Paris and slipped the Dale Carnegie jacket over it so people wouldn't stare at me like some kind of pervert."

He held the book up, like a preacher waving the Bible. "You must read this, and read it soon," he said. "It's part of a trilogy that I think is invaluable to any person who has ever thought of becoming an artist. And if that sounds boring, there's a nice raunchy sex scene every three or four pages to keep things moving along. Let me find the passage I want you to read."

He flipped through the pages until he found the correct one, then put the book in Carpo's hands and tapped a paragraph circled in faded pencil.

Every day we slaughter our finest impulses. That is why we get a heart ache when we read those lines written by the hands of a master and recognize them as our own, as the tender shoots which we stifled because we lacked the faith to believe in our own powers, our own criterion of truth and beauty. Every man when he gets quiet, when he becomes desperately honest with himself, is capable of uttering profound truths. We all derive from the same source. There is no mystery about the origin of things. We are all part of creation, all kings, all poets, all musicians; we have only to open up, only to discover what is already there.

When Carpo finished reading, he handed the book to Jack, who was beaming with anticipation.

"It's a great piece, isn't it?" he asked. "I recite it every morning before I sit down to write. It's my morning prayer. And look, this is what I used for the memory marker, my boarding pass." Jack showed the Trans World Airways ticket stub that was saving the page. "Remember that passage, it's important. More important than anything the so-called critics will ever say about your dreams, your ideas, and your creations. Listen to your soul. If you follow what's in there, it'll always be a masterpiece."

Jack's unbridled enthusiasm made Carpo frown. It sounded so easy and attainable; he didn't believe that success could be that simple. "How will I be able to tell if what I'm creating is any good?"

Jack's smile disappeared, covered by the folds of an aging face. "That's easy, Carp, you don't know. Never. You will die not knowing, never sure if anything you've ever created is any good. If you have to know, then you shouldn't try to be an artist."

Carpo had typed the passage by Henry Miller onto file cards and tacked them to his cubicle in the newsroom and over his desk at home. Like Jack, he recited it every time he sat down to work. He may not have been a fiction writer, but he felt that if the adages were good enough for Henry Miller and Jack Crawford, they were good enough for him.

In any case, it was the memory markers that enabled him to confirm Jack's claim that he had read all the books in the cottage. Leafing through the pages, he had found ticket stubs from the movies and opera, business cards, dinner receipts, gnawed toothpicks, expired credit cards, discarded gum wrappers, postcards, and low denominations of foreign money. The markers transformed each book into a mini–personal diary, chronicling the places that Jack had visited and the people he had met during the time he had read the book. And every book on each of the shelves had scraps of Jack Crawford's life hanging from its pages.

Carpo finished his seltzer and set the plate and glass on the table. His eyes ran back over the bookshelves and photographs, feeling a surge of desperation. There wasn't enough time to pack it all, and even if there were, he didn't have the space to store it. Besides, it belonged here. In this dark, cluttered cave where Jack had created his art. To take it somewhere else would destroy its very essence.

Thinking about Jack's life and the cottage brought his conversation with Elizabeth Jessup to mind. She had claimed that she and Jack once had been next-door neighbors in another town. He couldn't recall Jack ever mentioning that he had lived outside of Bridgewater.

He carried his dishes to the kitchen, his mind straining to remember the name of the town that Elizabeth Jessup had mentioned. Something beginning with a "south," such as Southtown or Southplace.

Then he remembered it: *Southville.*

If anyone could help him learn about Southville, he figured it was his new contact at the New Milford Public Library. He looked up the library's number in the phone book and dialed it. When he was connected, he asked to be transferred to the reference desk, and Dorothy Elwes.

"Michael dear, how are you?" Dorothy announced warmly as if they had met thirty years, instead of three hours, ago. "I hope the information on Bridgewater was helpful this morning."

"It was Ms. Elwes. Very helpful."

"Please, call me Dorothy. I sound like your mother with that *Ms.* buzzing around in front of everything."

He smiled; Dorothy was old enough to be his grandmother. "I'll call you Dorothy if you call me Carpo. I prefer it to Michael."

"That's a deal. Now, what can I do for you?"

"I've come across something that seems to be linked to Jack Crawford's past. It's a town in Connecticut by the name of Southville. Do you know where it's located."

"Do you mean Southbury? There's a town by that name a little north of here."

He racked his brain, trying to remember what Elizabeth Jessup had called the town. "No, I'm almost positive it was Southville. I think Jack lived there about forty years ago."

"That might explain my ignorance. I moved to New Milford only ten years ago. But why don't you give me a day to poke through the state archives, see what turns up."

Carpo recited the phone number at the cottage and told

Dorothy to call if she learned anything. No sooner had he replaced the phone to its cradle than it began ringing. Figuring it was another call from the press, he picked it up but didn't speak.

"Hello?" a woman asked. "Is someone there?"

It was Amanda. "Hi, it's Carpo," he said. "How are you?"

"Fine, thanks. Doing much better than I was this morning. Listen, if you're not busy already, I'd like to invite you over for dinner tonight. I want you to see my studio before the week is up."

His first impulse was to follow his bad feeling earlier in the day and say no. Unfortunately, his mouth had a mind of its own. "I'd love to, Amanda. What time should I come by?"

"Anytime after six is fine. It should still be light out, so we can have drinks on the patio before the mosquitos get us."

"Sounds great. Can I bring anything?"

"Just yourself. Actually, bring Floyd too. I miss him."

"It'll be the three of us, then."

"Great," she said, "I'm looking forward to seeing you."

"Me, too," he said shyly, noting how his heart was pounding. Because he *was* looking forward to seeing her. Very much.

Nine

A batch of star lilies had bloomed in the garden that after-noon; he thought they would make a nice present for Amanda. The trumpet-shaped flowers, edges tinged pink and red, lured dozens of clamoring honeybees. He carefully avoided the bees as he clipped a handful of the prettiest flowers, wrapping each stem in a moist paper towel to keep them fresh.

They started for Amanda's on foot, heading up the long driveway to Beach Hill Road. The concept of walking to a neighbor's house excited him, being accustomed to taking the bus or the subway to get anywhere in the city. Floyd seemed just as eager for the excursion. He trotted ahead, nose to the ground, inspecting every animal track and fecal dropping they crossed. There was plenty to inspect: deer hooves, turkey toes, raccoon fingers, and even a flattened toad were all preserved in the dirt surface. Floyd tested each one for freshness. A few proved so recent, he charged into the underbrush to see if he could catch them.

Amanda's house, a small gray saltbox with chimneys poking up at opposite ends of the roof, was a quarter-mile down Skyline Ridge Road. It was an old house, something that Carpo could determine from the number over the front door. Because of Bridgewater's small size and relative paucity of homes, the post office used the date that the house was built as its street number. Thus, Jack's address was 1955 Beach Hill Road, referring to the year he completed the cottage. The saltbox was an incredible 1797 Skyline Ridge Road, making it one of the oldest houses in town.

He knocked the hefty brass knocker against the front door; it struck the wood like a battering ram, sending a boom deep inside the house. After a moment, Amanda appeared. She was dressed in a black skirt and a cream-colored linen blouse, top three buttons undone, sleeves rolled up, and a smidgen of flour on her cheek. She smiled at him with a grin so warm and infectious, it instantly melted his inhibitions.

"Carpo, this is wonderful," she said, shaking his hand between the two of hers. "Please come in. Make yourself at home."

"These are for you," he said, presenting the lilies. As she sniffed them, he turned and whistled for Floyd, who was busy watering the base of an oak tree.

"Thank you, these are beautiful. Oh, and hello to you too, Floyd." She knelt to the dog's level, enduring a barrage of licks, one that erased the spot of flour. "What can I get you guys?"

"What are you having?"

"Nothing yet. Though I'm thinking of champagne, if you're in the mood."

"That sounds great. My partner here will stick with plain old water."

She carried the flowers into the kitchen, giving him a chance to look over the interior, an open space loosely divided into three areas. He was standing in the living room, where a white couch faced a stone fireplace. The dining area was behind the couch, denoted by a long, wood table set for two. The kitchen was shielded from view by a six-foot-high brick wall; over the top he could see a row of tarnished brass pots hanging from hooks in the ceiling. The decorations in the room were eclectic: antiques mixed with art deco, landscape paintings hanging beside abstract paintings. He felt immediately that he was in the nest of an artist.

"So how've you been?" Amanda called from the kitchen.

"I've been busy. Jack's family is putting the cottage on the market and I offered to sort through his belongings. There's so much to do, I hardly know where to begin."

"If I can help with anything, just tell me." She reappeared with a bottle of Taittinger, two champagne flutes, and a vase with the lilies. She put the lilies in the center of the table, then handed him the bottle. "You do the honors."

He unpeeled the gold foil, then twisted the cork from the bottle with a terrific pop; Floyd flinched as if he'd been shot. He splashed champagne into the flutes, then they clinked glasses and sipped.

"Tell me," Amanda said, "have you decided what to do with Floyd?"

"I'm toying with the idea of bringing him back to New York with me."

"That's a wonderful idea."

"Yeah, we'll see. I've got to figure out how to make him comfortable there. My apartment is tiny, and it obviously doesn't have a backyard."

"Anything's better than giving him up to strangers." She

pointed at a set of doors behind the dining table. "Come on, let's go outside."

They stepped onto a moss-lined stone patio overlooking a spacious backyard about a full acre in size. The patio faced in the opposite direction from the patio at the cottage; the focus here on woods and wildlife as opposed to the reservoir and the steel bridge. At the back of the property, nestled in the fringe of the woods, sat a large, weathered barn.

"Is that where your studio is?" he asked.

"That's it, just sitting there reminding me of all the work I have to do."

He made a sweeping motion with his arm, taking in the cottage, the backyard, and the barn. "God, you've got a great setup here. You're lucky to live so close to the place where you work. You must get a ton of work done."

"It's perfect: quiet, private, and lots of room. It's a complete one-eighty from my apartment in New York."

"You lived in the city?"

"For six years, down in SoHo. Basically I lived in a closet, generously called a studio. The real estate agent claimed the place got morning light. He was right. Only problem is, it had to seep down a six-story air shaft to reach me."

He laughed at the image. "Were you painting then?"

"Yes, but not professionally. I was taking classes at the School of Visual Arts." She rolled her eyes. "New York is one heck of an expensive place to try and make it as an artist."

"How did you end up here?"

"I grew up here."

"In this house?"

"No, my parents had a place on Route 133, closer to the center of town."

"Where do they live now?"

"They're divorced. My dad lives in Roxbury, and my mom lives in Florida." Amanda swirled her champagne around the glass. "How about your folks?"

Her question made him wish that he hadn't brought up the topic. "They live in Los Angeles," he said, leaving out the fact that he hadn't spoken to his father in more than four years.

"Is that where you grew up?"

"No, I was born in Manhattan and raised in Roslyn, Long Island."

"And where do you live now?"

"Twelfth Street, between Second and Third."

"That's the East Village, right? I love that area, it's the coolest part of the city. And it's probably the last place a real artist can afford to live."

He shook his head. "Unfortunately, it's getting very gentrified. They cleaned up Tompkins Square Park a few years ago, and just last year Starbucks and the Gap opened stores on Second Avenue. It almost set off riots."

She shook her head. "I swear, it seems like every neighborhood in the country has the same five chain stores. It's so boring."

"I'm afraid it's here to stay," he said. "Tell me more about Bridgewater. Has it always been your home?"

"I've always called it home, but I did move away for about ten years. It's strange to be back, especially since all I wanted when I was growing up was to move away from here."

"Why?"

"I hated it. Bridgewater is small, conservative, and bor-ing. That's probably why I love it now. I can finally get some work done."

"But don't you miss parts of the city? It seems like such an integral part of the art world. All the galleries, and muse-ums, and artists."

"I still visit. And besides, the New York art scene isn't all it's cooked up to be. Most of those alleged artsy types care less about the art than the scene. It's easy to get swept up in it all—who is, who's not, who's in, who's out. Sorry, but I don't want to spend my life criticizing other people's careers. I want to have my own career."

"That reminds me of Jack. He used to grouse about peo-ple who claimed they wanted to be a writer but never did any writing. In New York there's a million writers' conferences, courses, and workshops, but the plain fact is, unless you start pushing some lead across the paper, nothing will ever get written."

She held her glass to her eyes, squinting through the rows of bubbles. "I still can't believe it about Jack. Especially the suicide. He seemed so happy to me, so at peace with himself. Don't you think it's odd that he didn't leave a note?"

She lowered the glass and stared at him, her magnetic eyes demanding a response. He felt a strong urge to tell her the truth, to tell her everything he had learned about Jack, Elizabeth Jessup, and the six others. Instead, he asked, "Amanda, have you ever heard of a town called Southville?"

The question seemed to catch her off guard. Panic swept through her eyes, turning the soft blue orbs into hard, cold marbles. She blushed and looked at the ground. "Why do you ask?"

Her reaction surprised him; suddenly, he was glad he hadn't told the truth. "I was going through some of Jack's personal effects and found a letter that mentioned it," he said nonchalantly. "I thought I'd ask you about it."

"No, I've never heard of it." She threw back her glass and drained the remaining liquid. "I'm going to get more champagne. I'll be right back."

She was gone for several minutes. When she returned, bottle of Taittinger in hand, she seemed calmer, though she still avoided eye contact as she refilled his glass. When she was done, she set the bottle on the patio. "Let's go to the barn."

As they started across the lawn side by side, their hands brushed together. He thought the contact was accidental, but then her hand slipped into his, fingers knitting together. It confused him to be racked by doubt and suspicion of her, and yet still be very much attracted to her.

Relax, he thought. *You've got a beautiful woman leading you by the hand to an empty barn. Just go for the ride.*

They entered through a door in the rock foundation. It felt as if they were stepping inside the hull of a drydocked whaling ship, an immense, dark space that no longer served its original purpose. The basement was cool and smelled of packed earth and rotting wood. There were also hints of other smells: sweet hay, dusty animals, and old manure.

They moved slowly through the darkness, feeling their way past rows of abandoned stalls. Light filtered through cracks in the low ceiling. Floyd followed behind them, sniffing at the haunted smells. Carpo called for him twice, but the dog paid no attention. Finally, they left him behind.

At the back of the basement they started up a flight of stairs, the steps so short and rickety that his feet banged against them. At the top she opened the door and they entered the body of the barn, a hulking space, roof thirty feet high, supported by thick wood beams that distorted the echoes of their footsteps.

She squeezed his hand and released it, then crossed to the closest wall. He heard something click, then hum as rows of halogen spotlights on the ceiling began to glow. The lights allowed him to see the far end of the barn, where a painting was hung.

It was a large painting, as big as any Carpo had ever seen. The frame measured about twenty feet high by fifteen feet wide, and it was attached to the center beam by an elaborate pulley system. Steel scaffolding stood at the side, from which he guessed she painted.

"It's huge," he whispered. Then, after he'd had a chance to see what it was, he added: "My God, Amanda, it's amazing."

It was a flower. A vibrant yellow sunflower painted from halfway up the stem to the top of its enormous, seed-filled head. Each seed in the flower—every bump, angle, and imperfection—was painted in detail. Incredible detail. Detail so exact and so obsessive that he could see the flower only in parts, as if he were inspecting it through the limited view of a microscope. He longed to put the painting outside, where he might stand back from it, fifty or more yards, and see the sunflower as a complete unit. Instead, he stepped closer, seeking out the brushwork that had created it. He noticed that the canvas was divided into small squares, two inches by two inches, and each square was filled with dozens of colors, dabs of pigment, and swipes of chroma, all of which somehow meshed together to form a recognizable image.

Amanda was behind him; he could smell her perfume, fresh and feminine, amid the stale odors of the barn. He turned to her and shook his head side to side to relay his admiration, since the words that came to mind to describe how much he liked the painting seemed grossly inadequate.

"I've been working on it for two months," she said, smiling. "I almost gave up on it twice, but now I think I'm going to finish it."

Head still shaking, he said, "You *must* finish it, Amanda. It's incredible."

"You really like it? I'm glad. Sometimes I get so wrapped up in my work, I have trouble knowing if it's accessible."

"Accessible? Who cares if it's accessible. It's a masterpiece. Really. It's one of the most amazing paintings I've ever seen."

She giggled at his passion, then squeezed his hand. "I think I'm really starting to like you. Want to see another one?"

"I'd love to."

She walked to the spot where she had turned on the lights. Next to the switch was a silver box. She lifted the cover and pressed a button. Suddenly, the sunflower shivered to life and the pulley system dragged it along the beam, toward them. Carpo stepped aside, letting it pass, then looked at the canvas behind it.

The frame was roughly the same dimension, but the subject of this painting was a rose. A giant rose with petals that stretched like red schooner sails, and thorns that curved like silver rhino tusks. A different pulley rattled to life, dragging the rose from the shadows, where he could see it better.

Again the mastery was in the detail. Detail so painstaking and exact that it had to be false. The flower's petals stretched eight feet wide; he could see how the light played on each pore in the surface. At the center of the flower, the petals swirled tighter and tighter, until they ended at a two-foot section of total black. Only, he had never seen a blackness with so much color, created from splashes of purple, crimson, orange, and green.

She returned to his side and held his hand again. He was conscious of her touch, the curious strength in her slender fingers, the same fingers that had created these astonishing works. He wanted to kiss her so badly, he felt dizzy. "You are amazing," he said. "I thought you'd be good, but I never expected this good."

"No, really, I'm not. You think I am because you're seeing something new, but this isn't as difficult as it looks."

"I think they're unsurpassed. And I'm sure other people are just as impressed."

"I don't show them to many people."

"Why not? They're better than half the things that get shown in museums these days. Most of those paintings are scribbles and splashes. These are works of art."

Her mouth twisted downward. "You're very sweet, but it's not true. All art has its reasons, even things that just look like scribbles."

"Then what is it?"

She stepped back and looked at him, considering her

response. "I think art must have a theory behind it. Even if the theory is just art for art's sake, there must be a central reason behind it. Sometimes I feel my paintings lack that."

"Do you show your work anywhere besides Kent?"

"I've sent slides to a few places in New York. No takers yet. One place wanted the rose, but they asked me to cut the canvas down. The size is my favorite part."

He pointed at the scaffolding. "And I guess you paint from that?"

"Yes, I roll it to whatever part of the canvas I'm working on."

"Would you be disclosing any trade secrets if I asked how you capture all that detail?"

"Nothing the next painter doesn't know. I start by taking photos of the subject I'm going to paint, and then I make sketches, in different lighting and from different angles. When I feel like I know the subject, really understand its essence, I divide the canvas into a grid, project an image on it, and begin painting."

"So it's not like you carry a flower up there and paint from it."

"I do take flowers up there, in fact I took some of those sunflowers I clipped yesterday morning, but I don't paint from one specific flower. I just use them for ... let's say, subtle inspiration. I need the photo projection so I can preserve the image during the weeks it takes to complete a painting."

He motioned around the cavernous room. "Seeing the size of your paintings, I can understand why your studio in SoHo didn't work out."

"You wouldn't believe what it was like living there. I

had to step sideways like this"—she turned her body to a profile—"just to fit through the door. I love it here: the peace, the high ceiling, the sense of space. I feel like the more space I have, the more room there is for my ideas to fly around."

He shook his head. "I couldn't work here."

"Why not?"

"I need to work in tight places. It's the opposite of you, I guess. I need to feel like I'm in a spot where my ideas can't escape. Maybe it's womb envy or something. I like to write in dark, cramped spaces."

"Womb envy? God, I haven't heard that since tenth grade. If that's womb envy, then I must suffer from penis envy, since I like everything so big."

He felt his face heat up; she looked at him and giggled. "Sweetheart, you're blushing. That's so cute. I embarrassed you."

"No, no, I'm not embarrassed," he said in a voice exaggeratedly deep. "I always have beautiful women speak about phallus size in my presence."

She punched him playfully in the arm. "There's one more canvas behind the rose. Can I show it to you?"

"I'd love to see it."

"This one's a little different from the others. I painted it when I first moved back to Bridgewater, before I started working on the flowers. It's actually based on a piece of folklore from this area."

"Roll 'er out."

She returned to the silver box; the pulley system rattled back to life and the giant rose whisked toward Carpo.

Later, when he'd had a chance to sort out what happened,

he was thankful that she had not been standing at his side as the rose rolled by. It prevented her from seeing the expression of shock on his face as the next painting emerged from the shadows.

The new painting depicted a doorway. The vantage point originated in a pitch-black room and faced another room, one that was brightly lit. A single band of light fell across the floor of the dark room, uniting the light and dark sections of the painting. The scene was the same as the one that had appeared in his dream the night after Jack's death. The only thing missing was the image of his father and Jack Crawford seated at the dinner table.

Amanda had perfectly replicated his nightmare.

Ten

It took him about a minute to recover from the shock of seeing that painting hanging from the roof of the barn. Amanda was still behind him, so she couldn't have known the extent to which it had affected him. To ensure that she didn't find out, he bit his lower lip and approached the painting.

The scene was executed on a smaller canvas than the previous two paintings, roughly ten feet high by five feet wide. Most of the canvas was painted black, utilizing the same variety of colors that had appeared in the center of the rose. The only light area was the narrow band that represented the fall of light through the doorway. It split the canvas down the middle, from top to bottom, with shades of yellow, blue, and white.

Despite the simplicity of the composition, the painting displayed the same obsession for detail that he had noticed in the previous works. Subtle wood grain patterned the surface of the door, a small dent marred the side of the brass knob, and the ribbons of light that seeped through the door's inner crack created a tiny reflection on the round metal hinges.

Before his silence became too obvious, he said, "So tell me what piece of folklore this is based on."

She walked toward him, her voice and footsteps echoing in the rafters. "It's not really a story or anything. I guess you could call it a belief. Some of the older people in town believe in a phenomenon called 'the doorway.' It's supposedly a passageway that we use at birth and death, sort of like an entrance and exit to the afterlife. Apparently, they believe it's important to pass cleanly through this doorway without getting trapped in between."

Remembering what Elizabeth Jessup had told him about the doorway, he nodded at the painting and asked, "Which one is this?"

"What do you mean?"

"Is it an entrance or an exit? Or trapped?"

She hesitated before answering. "In my heart I think it's an entrance, since that would signify a birth. But someone else might see it as representing death or as trapped. I purposely made it ambiguous. Have you heard of this legend before?"

"No."

"I learned it from Bethie Jessup. She used to say that when a doorway gets stuck, it means a person is trapped between worlds. She had a name for it: a ripple. She also had all sorts of theories about what caused doorways to become stuck."

He stared at the painting in silence, too disturbed to comment further. He wondered why every time he allowed himself to trust Amanda, she said or did something that triggered alarm bells in his head.

His thoughts were interrupted by Floyd, who began

howling in the basement. He threw his hands up in a show of exasperation, even though he was thankful for the interruption. "I'd better check what's wrong."

He jogged to the stairs and descended to the basement level. He couldn't see Floyd in the darkness, but he could hear him. The dog was whining in one of the stalls, claws scratching against something that sounded like wood.

"Floyd, knock it off," he shouted.

Figuring the dog was trying to dig up a mouse nest, he felt blindly through the darkness until he located his collar, then he hauled him out of the barn. Amanda's face appeared in one of the windows; she motioned for him to wait outside. Carpo found a stick and started tossing it to Floyd. A minute passed before the barn lights turned off, then another minute, and Amanda emerged from the basement.

"Don't you lock that?" he asked, noticing that she had only swung the door shut.

"Why? There's nothing of value in there."

"What about your paintings?"

She brushed off his concern with a nonchalant wave of her hand. "They're fine," she said. "It's not like someone can run away with one."

As they crossed the lawn, he noticed how fast dusk was falling. Tree shadows reached halfway to the house and a tiny black bat flapped back and forth between the barn and the woods. Through the trees a full moon hugged the horizon.

"Hungry yet?" Amanda asked when they reached the patio.

"Starving. What's on the menu?"

"It's a surprise," she said with a mischievous grin, then opened the door to the house.

As soon as he stepped inside, his nose encountered the surprise: a tantalizing aroma of home-cooked food that set his stomach growling like a chain saw. After instructing him to sit at the table, Amanda disappeared into the kitchen. She emerged a moment later with a basket of bread and a mixed green salad topped with walnuts and goat cheese. She placed both in front of him, then grabbed a bottle of wine from an ice bucket on the sideboard and filled their glasses.

He waited for her to sit before reaching inside the bread basket; it was black bread with raisins, that luring combination of grain and sweetness, and best of all, it was warm. He ripped off a hunk and spread it with butter, then heaped salad on his plate and began eating.

A minute passed before he realized that Amanda was watching his ravenous consumption, a smile splashed across her face. Mouth full of food, he covered it with his napkin and mumbled, " 'Scuse me."

"Please, Carpo! Keep eating. I'm glad you're enjoying it. Nothing's worse than dinner guests who don't eat."

"No worries about that," he said, then he reached for a second helping of bread.

When Amanda brought out the next course, he wished he had not taken that second helping of bread; Cornish game hens baked with a tangy apricot glaze, garlic and rosemary roasted potatoes, and steamed fresh asparagus. He ate slower now, intent on pacing himself through the remainder of the meal.

When his plate was scraped clean, thanks to a third helping of bread, he pushed back his chair and stared at her.

She was leaning back too, knees propped on the edge of the table, wineglass cupped in her hands.

"How do you paint?" he asked.

She cocked her head. "What do you mean?"

"I'm curious about what it's like in the barn when you're working? The atmosphere. For instance, do you play music?"

"Oh, no, music would be a distraction. I prefer absolute silence." She tapped her forehead. "It doesn't compete with what's going on in here."

"What do you wear?"

She rolled her eyes. "You wouldn't happen to be a journalist, would you?"

"It's not that. I'm just trying to imagine how you look while you paint."

She ran her fingers through her hair, twisting it into a long bundle which she curled over one shoulder. "I wear a T-shirt, a pair of dungarees, and an old apron. I tie my hair up, out of my face, and I go to work. Oh, and I smoke. A lot. I seem to think better when there's smoke swirling around my head."

"You're a smoker? I never imagined."

"Goes against my wholesome image, right?"

"No, it's just that I've never seen you smoke."

"I don't smoke much. Half a pack a day at the most."

"It doesn't bother me. In fact, if you have some, I'll join you for one."

"Now I'm the one who's surprised." She pulled a pack of Camel lights from a drawer in the sideboard, knocked out a cigarette, then tossed the pack to him. After they had both lit up, she said, "Let's turn the tables here. How do you write?"

"Poorly."

She frowned. "Why do you always downplay what you do? Like the first day I met you, you insisted that you weren't even a writer."

"Because I'm not."

"Yes, you are."

"I write, but I'm not a writer."

"I don't see the distinction."

"A writer is someone who writes something that people can read. The stuff I write gets read by two people, the anchors at Channel 8, and that's it. Not exactly what I'd call a big audience."

"But think of all the people you reach. What are your station's ratings?"

"We did a seven in the last sweeps."

"How many people are a seven?"

"It's about half a million homes."

"Half a million! That's incredible, Michael. I'll bet that's more than any book Jack ever sold. And you do that every night."

"You can't compare them. What Jack did is permanent. Walk into any bookstore or library in the country and his words will be there. Probably forever. My stuff gets written, read, and discarded, all in the same day."

She squinted, he couldn't tell whether from the cigarette smoke or something else. "If it bothers you so much," she said, "why don't you write a book?"

"About what?"

"I don't know."

"You can't just sit down and write a book. You've got

to have an idea." He flicked ash in the bread dish. "And you've got to be good."

"You certainly set the bar high."

"What do you mean?"

She stared at the ceiling, cigarette dangling from the side of her mouth. "Let's see: It has to be good, it has to be published, *and* it has to last forever. If I applied those same criteria to my painting, I'd never do anything. I'd freeze up every time I touched my paintbrush."

She took another puff, then crushed out the cigarette. "One time, Jack read me this incredible passage about artistic inspiration," she said. "It was by this writer whose works—"

"Henry Miller."

"Yeah, that's him. Did Jack read it to you too?"

"Yes. And I actually reread it this afternoon."

"I think it's good advice, Michael. Like you said on the patio, if you want to be a writer, you've got to start pushing lead across the paper sometime, whether or not it's any good."

He exhaled, exasperated. "I would love to be a writer, but I don't know what to write about."

"Seems pretty obvious to me. Write about Jack. You knew him as well as anyone else did."

He didn't answer, though the idea intrigued him. Not only did he know Jack as well as anyone else, he had access to all of Jack's papers and letters; the cottage was a repository of his entire life. If only he had more than a few days to sort through it all.

He took a final drag from his cigarette and stamped it

out. Amanda stacked her bread dish onto her plate and asked: "Any takers for dessert?"

He curled his hands over his stomach and moaned as if his belly ached. "I don't know if I can fit it."

"Don't worry, it's a light dessert."

A minute later an entire strawberry rhubarb pie appeared before him. It must have come straight from the oven; the steaming innards warped the flaky crust like bubbling lava. He closed his eyes and inhaled. "You win. I'll make room."

She handed him a knife and two plates. He sliced two enormous wedges, balancing each on the knife, and spilled them over to plates. When he took his first bite, his mouth salivated so fast, it hurt. The pie was baked to perfection: soft tart fruits complemented by a rich, buttery crust. A gush of emotion swept over him, and he exclaimed, "Amanda, you are extraordinary."

She grinned with amusement. "What do you mean by that?"

"You're an amazing artist, an incredible cook, a wonderful host. . . ." He paused, fork waiting to plunge back into the pie. "You know, it bothers me that Jack never talked about you. He was always telling me about the people in town. I can't believe he forgot to mention you."

"We didn't meet until I moved back to Bridgewater."

"But you grew up here. You must have run into him sometime."

She stared into the candle, the stark blue of her eyes surpassed only by the hottest part of the flame. He wondered what existed behind those cobalt windows. Even though there were things about her that made him uneasy, there was plenty that he liked. Perhaps that was why he waited so patiently for her response.

"My parents didn't like Jack. Especially my dad." Her eyes moved from the candle to Carpo. "My dad was born here, so he knew Jack growing up. He thought Jack was a snob, used to call him the affirmative-action artist. I think he resented Jack's success."

"That's nothing to be ashamed of. Lots of people didn't like Jack. He was a controversial person."

She exhaled nervous energy. "My dad's not . . . he's not exactly the most enlightened human being."

"Neither is mine," he said. "My dad and I haven't spoken to each other in four years."

Her face registered shock. "Four years, Michael, that's terrible. What happened?"

"We had a stupid argument one night and it sort of escalated into this major brouhaha. I don't know what to do about it."

"Why don't you call him?"

"I've tried. I called two years ago and he wouldn't take my call. He's stubborn, and so am I." He scraped the last of his pie onto the fork. "So, with all that water under the bridge, how did you and Jack end up becoming so friendly?"

"About five years ago I read a short story by Jack in *The New Yorker*. It made me cry, partly because it was so incredible, but mostly because I felt like I'd missed an opportunity to know someone as brilliant as him. When I moved back here, I made a point of introducing myself to him. Thank God I did, at least I got to know him for those two years. I'm lucky for that much."

Floyd moaned from beneath the table. Carpo peered over

the edge at him. The dog was in the midst of one of his nightmares, eyelids fluttering, muscles twitching. Carpo nudged him with his foot. "It's okay, Floyd, it's only a bad dream."

She walked over and knelt beside him. "Is he really having a nightmare? I didn't know dogs could dream."

"Sure they can. Look at the way his eyes are jumping beneath the eyelids."

She giggled. "What do you think he's dreaming about?"

"Probably something horrible, like serial-killer cats prowling Bridgewater, or an evil scientist poisoning cans of Alpo."

He nudged the dog harder. Floyd lifted his head and stared groggily at the two of them.

"Poor Floydie," Amanda cooed. "He's tired."

"Speaking of tired, what time is it?"

She glanced at her wristwatch. "It's a little past one."

"Gosh, I've got to get home. I was hoping to wake up early tomorrow and start sorting Jack's belongings."

They both stood; Floyd, sensing that they were about to leave, struggled to his feet. As they walked to the door, Amanda looped her hand through Carpo's. "I've really enjoyed your company," she said.

"Hold on, I'm not going anywhere until you let me clean up. The kitchen must be a mess."

"The kitchen is always a mess, I'll deal with it tomorrow. I have a dishwasher and all morning to do it."

"Are you sure?"

"Positive."

She opened the front door and allowed Floyd to slide

past them into the front yard. Carpo stepped out too, then felt a soft tug at his elbow.

"Hey," Amanda said coyly, "where you going so fast?"

There was a smile on her face, soft, relaxed, and amused. It influenced her entire expression, suspending the corners of her mouth, dimpling her cheeks, and tightening her eyes. He started to mumble something stupid about where he was going, when he noticed the shape of her mouth change. The smile drooped into a pout and she whispered: "Shhh." Then she placed her hand on the side of his chin and guided him close.

He watched her move toward him in parts, like staring at one of her paintings—clear blue eyes, perfect nose, moist, nut-brown lips. She looked beautiful, so much so, it stole his breath away. An instant before their mouths touched, he closed his eyes and relaxed.

The first kiss was a light stroke on the lips, as soft as a feather. She shifted to another spot on his face, the tip of his nose, then both his eyes and finally the lobe of his ear. His body slowed, breathing and heart rates settling to a rhythmic throb.

"Thank you," she whispered in his ear, his skin prickling from the humid words. "I've had a wonderful time tonight."

"Me too," he whispered back. "I want to see you again."

"Call me tomorrow. I'm here all day."

He nodded to show he would, then leaned forward and did the kissing, hard and concentrated on her mouth. Her lips separated, and when he experienced the warmth and wetness between them, he shivered. She felt his reaction, her mouth curling into a smile. His mouth followed, and soon they began laughing.

"I'll see you tomorrow," he said. "Good night."

As he walked down the path and started for home, he did a quick calculation of how many more hours until he could hold her in his arms and kiss her again. Tomorrow night seemed a lifetime away to him. And so did the next kiss.

Eleven

Eight-thirty the next morning, Dorothy Elwes called from the New Milford Public Library. She sounded hoarse and out of breath, as if suffering a touch of asthma. Even in his semi-awake state, Carpo sensed big news.

"Sorry to bother you so early, dear, but I found it. I've located Southville. It's a town . . . or, it was one . . . a tiny town, not far from here. In fact, you'll never believe where it is."

"Tell me, Dorothy, where?"

She took a deep breath—by the sound of it, she needed one—then said, "There isn't time. We open in fifteen minutes, I haven't stacked returns, and there's a group of children coming in for a reading. Can you come here instead? You're going to want to see this in person anyway."

He promised he would stop by the library as soon as he looked presentable. After hanging up the phone, he went into the bathroom, showered and shaved, then into the bedroom to dress. Unsure of where Dorothy's finding would lead him, he chose his clothes for comfort and utility: blue jeans, button-down oxford, and rubber-soled hiking boots. Before leaving he poured the entire carafe of coffee down the drain, turned off the machine, and tossed Floyd a biscuit.

Outside, thick gray fog hovered at the tree line, obscuring the sun and surrounding hillside. It forced him to soberly navigate the twists and turns of Route 133, the headlights on and two hands gripping the wheel. The woods looked like a tropical rain forest: tree trunks darkened from moisture, leaves sodden and droopy. Passing cars kicked mist on the windshield, which he cleared aside with the intermittent wipers.

When he reached New Milford, he circled the green three times before finding a parking spot, two blocks down from the library. The clock on the dashboard glowed nine-thirty; despite the bad weather, he had made it to the library within an hour of Dorothy's call.

He found her at the information desk, helping a boy scout look something up on the computer. He caught her eye and held his hands together like a book, then pointed at the periodicals section. While waiting, he wanted to check what was happening in New York.

Since his arrival in Bridgewater four days earlier, he hadn't been able to follow any local news. He felt completely out of touch, which, on a normal vacation, would have been a good way to feel. Of course, this was no normal vacation. He took his time flipping through the Big Three—*The Post*, *The News*, and *The Times*—scanning headlines—to see if he knew the stories—and noting bylines—to see if he recognized the reporters. Bylines beat out headlines three to one.

"You got here fast," Dorothy said.

She was standing beside him, arms folded, waiting for him to finish reading. He folded the newspapers and returned them to the shelf.

"What did you find, Dorothy?"

She shook her head, finger to her lips. "Let's go to the study room. It's in there."

As they crossed the library, Dorothy picked a key from the dozens attached to the chain on her waist. She unlocked the study room and turned on the overhead. He immediately noticed the stack of newspaper articles on the desk. She went to the desk, grabbed the top page on the stack, and handed it to him. "This," she said confidently, "should answer all your questions about Southville."

He looked at the article; a photocopy taken from microfilm of *The New Milford Times*, dated 1955. The copy machine had badly distorted the article's faint newsprint, but it hadn't dimmed its message:

SOUTHVILLE RESIDENTS LOSE BATTLE FOR TOWN

by Joshua L. Stringer, Staff Writer

Hartford, January 4, 1955 — After an epic seven-year David vs. Goliath legal fight, the final 12 residents of Southville, Connecticut, have lost their last bid to rescue their town from a planned hydroelectric power plant.

On Tuesday, State Supreme Court Justice Vincent W. Arresman ruled that the Connecticut Light and Power Company could proceed with construction of the 13-million dollar Shepaug Valley dam. The project, which will create a narrow reservoir along the Housatonic Valley, will submerge the enclave of Southville. C.L.&P. administrative vice president Robert T. Grundy hailed the decision as "a major step toward providing cheap, reliable electricity to the forty thousand New Milford area residents." Mr. Grundy also outlined a plan to hire a Canadian lumberjack crew to clear the valley of trees and brush by the end of spring, speeding Southville's demise.

Justice for Southville, an organization representing the final 12 residents of Southville, has vowed to appeal the ruling. Its spokesman, Negro columnist Jack Crawford, characterized Judge Arresman's decision as "pathetically stupid." Mr. Crawford accused local and state officials of conducting a "campaign of political, social, and economic terror" against the residents of Southville.

Mr. Grundy refused to comment directly on the accusations. He says that a trust fund established by C.L.&P. would "adequately and satisfactorily compensate those residents displaced by the Shepaug dam project."

After he finished the article, Carpo read it again to make sure he understood everything in it, then looked at Dorothy. There was a strange expression on her face; she looked pale and rigid, as if her skin were made of plastic. When she spoke, her voice sounded ragged.

"I've lived here ten years, been a librarian eight of them, and I've never heard of Southville. This whole time I thought you had to be mistaken, that you really meant Southbury and just got the names mixed up. Now, it turns out, all along it's me who's wrong."

He stared at her, wondering why this point had made her so upset. She motioned to the rest of the pile. "See it for yourself. It's a little tedious at times, but it's all there, the whole story. I sorted it according to date, so it'll unfold just as it happened. Find me at the reference desk when you're finished."

He followed her to the door. "Thanks, Dorothy. This goes way beyond the call." She looked at him, face blank, and then her eye twitched. Or was it just a blink? He couldn't tell.

"I just hope it's useful for your . . . a-hem . . . news story."

She turned and abruptly crossed the library; he stayed at the door, watching her go, wondering: *Why did she clear her throat like that? Has she seen past my working-reporter alibi that easily?*

He went to the desk, pulled a notebook and pencil from his knapsack, and set to work. He started with the first article on the pile, the one he had read twice, and worked his way down. When he reached a significant story, he wrote the date and a quick summary of its contents. He moved from one article to the next without pausing or lifting his head, working until the entire stack had shifted from his left side to his right side, and he knew all there was to know about the long-forgotten town of Southville, Connecticut.

The second to last article in the pile, dated November 14, 1959, came from *The New York Times*, a good indication of how big the Southville story had become. He scribbled one word in his notes to summarize it: *Victory!* The date was significant to Jack, significant to the members of Justice for Southville, and, as he had just learned, significant to many others.

On that day in Washington, D.C., a federal appeals court

judge reversed two lower court rulings to find Bridgewater, Brookfield, and the county's main power supplier, C.L.&P., guilty of conspiracy against the town of Southville. As part of the restitution, the judge ordered that each member of Justice for Southville receive an immediate ten-thousand-dollar cash payment. Of much more significance, the judge also named the twelve members as rightful heirs to the land beneath Lake Lillinonah.

Now Carpo understood why Dorothy had looked so shell-shocked. Forty years ago, the Southville ruling had been big news. Big enough to garner attention in a national newspaper. How *was* it possible she had never heard of Southville?

He flipped to the final article in the stack: a black and white photograph that had accompanied an article about the November 14 ruling in *The New Milford Times*. The photograph showed the twelve members of Justice for Southville celebrating their victory on the steps of the federal courthouse. Hats flying, faces beaming, fists raised in power salutes, it was a moment of pure, spontaneous euphoria captured on film.

He stared at each face in the photograph, checking to see if he recognized anyone. There was Jack, nattily dressed in a three-piece suit with a gold fob, bow tie, and a gray fedora, a celebratory stogie jutting from his mouth. There was also Elizabeth Jessup, thinner and surprisingly pretty, he thought, with large brown eyes, a coy smile, and a saucy tilt to her hips. No one else looked familiar, so he checked the names in the caption. As soon as he finished reading the first row, his hands started shaking.

It can't be. He put the photo down and wiped his palms on his jeans, freaked out, thinking: *It can' t be true.*

Of the twelve names listed below the photograph, he recognized seven: Jack Crawford, Elizabeth Jessup, Claudell Jenkins, Karla Phelan, Charlie Simms, Frank Washington, and Charlotte Thigpen. They were the seven people whom he had found during his research earlier in the week, the same people who had died in Bridgewater the past two years of accidents or suicides.

It can't be true, he thought again, even though he knew it was. One by one someone was murdering the members of Justice for Southville.

Twelve

Carpo did not recognize the other five people in the Justice for Southville photograph: Jimmy Hunter, Camilla Tompkins, Fern Gimlins, Trent Donovan, and Artie Spellman. He scribbled their names into his notebook, then walked out to the reference desk to find Dorothy. She was kneeling beside the copy machine, pouring replacement powder into the printer cartridge.

"Dorothy, when you get a chance?"

She swiveled on her heel and stared up at him for a moment, then lifted a charcoal-smudged finger in the air, telling him to wait. She slammed the side panel on the machine and wiped her hands on a tissue. "So how did it turn out, dear?"

Her question seemed innocent enough, especially the offhand way in which she asked it, but he wasn't fooled. Just from the assortment of articles he knew that she had seen through his journalism alibi. The photograph alone proved that. Placed strategically at the bottom of the pile, it meant that she had stopped her research once she had discovered the link between the recent deaths in Bridgewater and the former residents of Southville. He was sure that she had seen the connection, but just in case he was wrong, he responded to her question with a noncommittal "It went fine."

They stood awkwardly in the tight space, looking everywhere but at each other. Dorothy made it easier when she whipped a handkerchief from her pocket and began to clean her glasses, breathing moisture onto the lenses and meticulously kneading them between her fingers. Finally, she mumbled, "So I guess you'll be wanting to find those other five next."

He exhaled, relieved. "You saw the connection, then. I was hoping you had."

She continued to polish the glasses. "Wasn't hard to see, between the research and the photo. It all kind of clicked."

"Do you understand why I couldn't tell you?"

She nodded as she tucked the handkerchief away and replaced her glasses. "Let's have a look again, make sure I've got all the names right." She pushed to the bottom of the pile and grabbed the photograph. "Let's see, Tompkins, Hunter, Gimlins, Donovan, and Spellman. Those would be the five, right?"

"Yes."

"Well, last night, seeing how I was already here doing research on it, I went ahead and checked the local census reports. Three of them are already dead, but I don't think it has anything to do with your ... story." She took out a piece of paper with notes written on it and read to him. "Jimmy Hunter died in 1982 of a heart attack, Artie Spellman died of colon cancer in 1987, and Camilla Tompkins died in 1993 of emphysema. Two years ago Trent Donovan moved out of Bridgewater. I checked postal records and tax returns, but I couldn't find a forwarding address." She looked up from the paper. "Unless I've overlooked someone, that leaves Fern Gimlins as the only member of Justice for South-ville still living in Bridgewater." She put the paper in his hand. Across the bottom was scrawled: *1922 Northrup Street.*

"Is this his address?" he asked.

"It was last May when they printed the phone book."

He felt a sudden urge to hug the librarian. "You're amazing, Dorothy. I owe you big-time."

She didn't respond or look at him. Instead, she removed her glasses and squinted at each lens, as if she intended to clean them again.

"Something wrong, Dorothy?"

"I haven't told you this yet," she said, "but I knew Jack Crawford. He was a friend. Last year, on my eightieth birthday, he donated five hundred dollars to the children's reading room in my name. Tell me the truth, Carpo. It wasn't a suicide, was it?"

"No, ma'am. I don't think it was."

"Then I must tell you something," she said, her voice trembling, "something very important."

He nodded to show he was listening.

"Three or four years ago a man came in here to do research on Bridgewater. I didn't pay much attention because he didn't want any help. One night while I was cleaning up, I found this photograph in the copy machine. I'm almost positive it's the same one, all those people celebrating on the courthouse steps."

"Are you sure it was his?"

"I think so."

"Who is he?"

"I never learned his name, but . . ."

"What, Dorothy?"

"He was a state trooper."

"A trooper!" Carpo exclaimed. "Do you mean a state trooper? Was it Trooper Walker from Bridgewater?"

"I don't know."

"Does he look like him?"

"I can't say for sure."

"If I had you meet him in person, would you be able to tell?"

She thought for a moment, then exhaled, frustrated. "I just don't know. It's so long ago, and I barely spent any time with him. The only thing I'm positive about is his uniform and that photograph."

He put Fern Gimlins's address in his pocket and snatched his knapsack off the desk. "It doesn't matter," he said, walking toward the door, "I know how to find out."

"How?"

"I'm going to ask him to his face."

Trooper Walker's squad car was missing from his driveway when Carpo reached Bridgewater. He circled the block, checking side roads to see if he could spot the silver cruiser, but it was gone. It might have been a blessing in disguise. He was so juiced by what he had learned at the library, he might have said something to Trooper Walker that he would end up regretting.

He stopped at the Village Store to buy a ham and cheese sandwich, a birch beer soda, and potato chips, then continued along Route 133 in the direction of the cottage. The heavy fog of the morning had cleared, replaced by a perfect blue sky. He turned off the air conditioner and lowered the windows. The whine of a lawn mower entered the car, as well as excited screams from the children playing kick ball behind the Burnham School. As he drove past the firehouse, he saw a work crew staking out the corners of a big red and white striped tent. A freshly painted sign explained what it was for: The Bridgewater Country Fair opened in one night.

He continued along Route 133, passing the street that led back to the cottage. He passed a small red water mill, then the road dipped alongside a white-water brook, tracing its contour. The trees created a thick canopy overhead; the air felt moist and cool. He hung his arm out the window and dried his palm on the wind.

After a quarter-mile the road widened. He could see the turnoff for Northrup Street two hundred feet away, and farther off, the Lillinonah bridge. As he put on his right-turn signal, he noticed a large dirt parking lot on the left side of the street. On a whim he steered hard left, pulling into the lot.

The lot was used as a loading and unloading ramp for pleasure boats on Lake Lillinonah. On the weekends it was filled to capacity, but on the weekdays—especially two o'clock on a Thursday—it was almost empty. Three pickup trucks with empty trailers were parked near the ramp. The breeze off the lake sent candy wrappers and empty beer cans sliding across the ground.

He parked by the water and turned the key backward in the ignition so the radio would run off the battery. He tuned it to News Radio 88, an all-news station from the city. The announcer's staccato delivery sounded as familiar as the stories she intoned: murders, fires, and bellicose one-liners by the mayor. He tilted the seat back, unwrapped his sandwich, and began to eat, eyes absorbing the view of the lake.

After he finished eating, he walked along the water's edge. A row of boulders ringed the shore, preventing people from loading their boats directly into the lake. He stood atop one of the rocks and peered into the shallows, trying to detect the spot where the bottom dipped into the valley. The sun hit the water at the wrong angle, making it impossible to see anything. He continued along the bank until he reached the edge of the lot, then walked a short distance on Route 133 and entered the pedestrian walkway on the bridge.

Though the sun was no longer overhead, the bridge radiated its heat. The macadam felt sticky underfoot, and a half-mile down the road, water mirages shimmered. The walkway took him down the left side of the bridge. Rusted steel work spread above his head like a giant spiderweb; when an occasional car whizzed by, the platform swayed like a rope bridge. He walked to the center of the span, roughly the middle of the lake, where he knew from his research the town of Southville had once existed.

The breeze was stronger here, whipping his hair and shirt, drying his sweat. The water surface was twenty feet beneath him and showed indications of a current. Submerged branches, leaves, and a plastic bag floated past. Near the bank, a fish ripple surfaced. Somewhere on this platform was the spot where Trooper Walker had found Claudell Jenkins's belongings: clothes, Reebok sneakers, and the suicide note. The railing on the edge came up to Carpo's waist, making it a simple barrier to vault. He leaned over the edge and stared into the lake. The water looked dark and silty;

the sun refracted into separate beams as soon as it split the surface. He tried to imagine what was farther down, all the way at the bottom: muck and detritus that had built up over the decades, entombing the scattered remains of Southville. It was an image that made him shiver.

Elizabeth Jessup was right, he realized, *this place is full of ripples.*

He felt a crazy urge to dive down there to the bottom of the lake, and see what, if anything, remained of the town. He fantasized about finding Southville still intact, a perfectly preserved Atlantis, looking exactly as it had back when Jack lived there.

He didn't hear the siren until he was almost off the bridge. It was moving toward him on Route 133, its undulating scream growing louder and louder, until Trooper Walker's squad car careened around the corner at a hundred miles an hour. He figured the trooper was headed to Brookfield, responding to an accident or crime, but a few hundred feet before the bridge the car swerved right, onto Northrup Street, tires squealing like a car chase in the movies.

As Carpo sprinted for his car, he realized what a terrible mistake he had made by stopping for lunch before driving to Fern Gimlins's house.

Thirteen

Carpo didn't need the street address to find Fern Gimlins's house anymore. Trooper Walker's squad car was parked on the front lawn of 1922 Northrup Street, the roof lights spinning with silent red and yellow flashes. He parked on the street and sprinted for the house, grimly noting that someone had left the front door open.

The house was built like a mobile home, narrow, metal siding, with three rooms all in a row. Inside, it looked as if a giant had picked up the unit and given it a violent shaking. Shards of glass sparkled on the floor amid shredded papers and broken furniture. His stomach started churning when he realized that the glossy black splatters on the wall were blood.

A voice came from the farthest room, a bedroom with stained walls and faded yellow curtains. In the dreary light, he could make out Trooper Walker kneeling over the body of Fern Gimlins.

When he got a look at the man, it dawned on Carpo that someone was beginning to panic. Whoever was killing the members of Justice for Southville seemed to have forgotten that the deaths were supposed to look like accidents or

suicides. Even Trooper Walker couldn't argue this one—
Fern Gimlins's throat had been slashed.

But when Trooper Walker started pounding on the man's
chest, pleading for him to keep breathing, Carpo realized
that the killer had made a second and much more serious
mistake: Fern Gimlins wasn't dead yet.

Trooper Walker whirled at the sound of his footsteps,
eyes venomous. "Christ, you scared me." Carpo thought he
was about to be ordered off the premises, as would have
happened at a New York City crime scene, but instead, the
trooper said, "Get over here and help me, he's still alive."

He knelt beside the trooper, averting his eyes from the
man's wrecked throat. "What can I do?"

"Hold his hand and talk to him. Try to keep him going.
I've got to see where the goddamn ambulance is."

Panic surged through him; he did *not* want to be left
alone with a dying man. Before he could protest, Trooper
Walker jogged from the room.

He looked at the man's face; the eyes were half closed,
pupils swimming beneath the lids, as if pleading to him for
help. He forced himself to look lower. When he saw the
slash, he wondered why Trooper Walker had bothered to
run to his car. Ambulance or no ambulance, Fern Gimlins
was on his way out.

He took the man's hand anyway and squeezed it. He
nearly screamed when the fingers responded, curling around
his palm. Fern's eyes flapped open and a horrible sound
escaped his throat, a sucking noise that reminded Carpo of
a sliced vacuum hose. Shiny black bubbles sputtered from
the wound. He squeezed the hand tighter. "Stay with me,

Fern. Come on, you can do it. Squeeze my hand. Help will be here in a second."

The man's eyes narrowed and a violent shudder passed through him, from his chest to his outer extremities. Carpo thought it was the death rattles, but then the man's body shifted, rolling to the side, as if he intended to get off the floor.

"No, Fern, stay still. Help is coming."

Fern stopped moving, but his hands came up and latched on to Carpo's wrists. The man's lips began to flutter and a faint sound came through them, a noise that might have formed words if the man's voice box hadn't been severed.

"It's okay, Fern. It's okay."

Fern tugged on Carpo's wrists, pulling him toward his mouth, his lips still moving.

"What is it? Are you trying to speak?"

Fern nodded slightly, then closed his eyes and shuddered again. He released his wrists and grabbed the side of his neck, guiding him closer. When Carpo's face was two inches from the man's mouth, a noise came through. It was a strange noise, a high whisper that sounded as if the words had traveled a hundred miles to get there. "A snow dam" was what it sounded like. "A snow dam."

Fern's hands quaked against Carpo's neck, but the lips remained steady, muttering the same thing over and over: "A snow dam. A snow dam."

Footsteps entered the house, two pairs. Then Trooper Walker shouted for someone to go to the bedroom. Fern must have heard them too, because his head lifted off the ground until his lips were brushing Carpo's ear. The words were faint, but clearer. He wasn't saying "A snow dam," Carpo realized, he was saying, "I know them."

"Who, Fern? The people who did this to you?"

Before Carpo could learn anything else, a hand yanked him roughly backward and Trooper Walker barked: "Give him air!"

Carpo stumbled back on his heels; a young paramedic toting two cases of equipment filled his space. He tried to stand over the man and watch, but Trooper Walker's hand stayed latched to his shoulder. "I want a word with you, Carpo," the trooper said ominously. "Right now."

They walked through the house, out the front door. An ambulance was parked beside the squad car on the lawn, and a second paramedic rushed past them, rolling an oxygen tank and other equipment. Two cars had pulled over at the curb, passersby who had stopped to gawk at the emergency vehicles and flashing lights.

When they reached the squad car, Trooper Walker stopped and folded his arms over his body, an impenetrable wall of muscle. "What the hell are you doing on Northrup Street?" he demanded.

"I was at the boat launch eating lunch when I heard your siren. I figured it had something to do with all the other deaths in town, so I followed you."

The trooper squinted at Carpo, teeth bared. "I'm starting to wonder about you. You've been here all of . . . what?— five days?—and I've got three bodies in town."

"Are you accusing me of that?"

"Well, it begs an answer how you got here so fast. I wasn't in that house thirty seconds before you showed up."

"I told you, I heard your siren." Carpo clenched his teeth,

furious that the trooper would accuse him of murder. It made him angrier when he remembered what Dorothy had found. "And before you start pointing fingers, there's something you should explain too."

The trooper glared pure hatred. "Like what?"

"Like why you went to the New Milford Library two years ago and made a copy of the photograph showing all twelve members of Justice for Southville. The same members, I might add, who've been dying in *your* town for the past two years."

The statement punched some of the hot air out of the trooper. He unfolded his arms and wiped his brow. "Yeah, I did some research," he admitted, "but it wasn't for no murder plot. I was just keeping track of secret organizations in this area."

"Secret organizations?" Carpo smirked. "How secret can Justice for Southville be if you can read about it in the newspaper?"

Trooper Walker shrugged. "Hold on a sec, I never made a copy of that photograph, I just took down the names of the members so I could keep track of them."

"A fine job you've done of it. So fine, there's nobody left." Carpo started across the lawn, heading for his car.

"I'm not done yet," the trooper shouted. "I still want some answers from you."

Carpo opened the door to his car. "You know where I'm staying."

"But you're not to leave town. Hear me? That's an order."

"I'm not going anywhere." Carpo smiled, upper lip curled with contempt. "Not until I find the person who's doing this. That's a promise."

He slid behind the steering wheel and started the motor. When he pulled away from the curb, he stomped so hard on the accelerator the tires spat a rooster tail of sand and gravel.

As he drove down the road, heading back to Route 133, he checked the rearview mirror. He saw Trooper Walker standing in the street, arms propped on hips, eyes lasering hatred after the car. He wasn't sure if it happened or not, but just before he disappeared around the corner he thought he saw a smile creep over the trooper's face.

He wasn't back at the cottage for forty-five seconds before he poured a glass of whiskey. He was shaking every-where, inside and out; he prayed the alcohol would deaden his nerves.

It didn't help matters when he spotted dried flecks of blood on his palms. He tried to scratch them off with his thumbnail, then walked into the bathroom to attack them with soap and water. When he glimpsed himself in the mir-ror, he was stunned to see a bloody palm print on his cheek. He filled the basin with water, as hot as he could stand it, and scrubbed his face and hands until his skin felt raw. While bent over the basin, he got a peek down his shirt. A trail of blood ran down his neck, below the collar. In a panic he pulled off his shirt and the rest of his clothes and crawled into the shower. He stayed there, soaking under the shower head, until every trace of Fern Gimlins had been rinsed from his body.

The whole time, Floyd stayed outside the bathroom, observing the antics from a crouched position, nose stopping exactly where the bathroom tile started. The dog waited patiently, watching Carpo dry and put on shorts and a T-shirt; every time Carpo looked at him, his tail thumped the ground, acknowledging the eye contact.

After throwing his clothes in the washing machine, Carpo headed to the porch, whiskey in one hand, portable telephone in the other. He was sure that Fern Gimlins had died after he left the bungalow; there wasn't a person on earth who could have survived the kind of injury he had suffered. That brought the tally to three deaths in five days. He felt hopeless to stop it, even though he knew who the next intended victim would be: Trent Donovan, the last surviving member of Justice for Southville.

He dialed the New Milford Public Library and asked to be transferred to the reference desk. Dorothy answered on the first ring. Without even identifying himself, he said, "It's happened again, Dorothy. They killed Fern Gimlins."

"Oh, dear," she gasped, as if the news had landed square in her gut. "Fern Gimlins is dead? Oh, my dear."

"I screwed up. On the way to his house I stopped for lunch. I should have gone straight over there. He was still alive when I got there. I might have saved him."

"That's plum silly, Carpo. There was no way of knowing he was in such immediate danger."

"You know they'll be going for Trent Donovan next. Dorothy, we've got to do something to find him—as fast as possible."

There was a pause from her end, then: "What do you mean *they?* That's the second time you've said it. Is more than one person responsible for this?"

"Fern Gimlins lived long enough to say he recognized the people who attacked him. He didn't name anyone or say how many, but he definitely said there was more than one person."

She cleared her throat. "I'm not sure how we can find this man ... Trent Donovan. I've checked all the records we have on hand. He moved out of Bridgewater a few years ago without leaving a change of address or a forwarding address."

"He must have kept in touch with someone around here. Maybe we can start that way. Talk to people whom he was friendly with in Bridgewater."

"I can find out a lot here, but not who someone was friends with. Anyway, it seems that all the people he'd be friendly with are dead now."

"But there's got to be someone who knows where he lives. People can't just disappear."

"I'll try my best, dear. I'll call some of the other libraries in the county and have them check their records. Roxbury, Washington Depot, Brookfield, Southbury, and Danbury are on the same system. Maybe something will turn up that way."

"Try it. Call me as soon as you find something. Okay, Dorothy? Anytime, day or night."

He hung up the phone and leaned against the Adirondack chair, sipping his drink. The alcohol was starting to speak to him, in its steady, depressing way. He could feel it seep through his limbs like a slow-moving poison. Out across the yard, the weather was mimicking his mood. The sun had retreated behind clouds again, huge black thunderheads that choked up the valley. He knew they signaled one of those late summer lightning storms that could light up the sky brighter than the Fourth of July.

All of a sudden he didn't feel like being alone. He didn't want to sit in the cottage and watch the flashes of lightning reflect on the lake, then count the seconds until the inevitable crack of thunder. He flicked the button on the side of the phone and retrieved the dial tone. He dialed from memory, not because he had used the number before, but because he'd been thinking about it the entire day. The phone rang twenty times before she answered: "Hello?"

His brain felt foggy from the drink, but it still sent a strong note of caution. For a second he couldn't think of anything to say.

"Hello?" she said again, less assertive. "Is someone there?"

He managed to whisper: "Amanda."

"Carpo? Is that you? What's the matter? You sound terrible."

"I'm okay, I guess. It's just that . . . I guess I could use a friend tonight."

"I'll be right there," she said, no hesitation. "You sit tight, I'm on the way."

Ten minutes after he had dropped the phone in his lap, a car sliced into the driveway. She knocked and let herself in; he was thankful, not feeling strong enough to get to the door. When she walked onto the patio, they didn't speak. She took one look at his face and went straight to him, wrapping her arms around his neck, pulling his head to her chest. She held him like that for a long time, tightly, as if he would fall if she released him. His eyes were closed, her hands stroking his face. From that position he could hear the inner machinations of her body: gurgles and rumbles in her stomach, inhales, exhales, and the round hypnotic thump of her heart.

She whispered things too. Nice things. Words that soothed his emotions like salve on a deep wound. The sorts of things he wished he had said to his father when he was younger, maybe even to Fern Gimlins before he died.

When the storm finally hit, she took him inside, bolting the patio door against the onslaught. Lightning exploded over the valley with dazzling phosphorescence, illuminating the yard as if it were daytime. The storm breathed life into the house; walls creaked, a loose shutter knocked, and tree branches dragged over the roof. Through it all was the sound of the rain, millions of drops that hammered the wood shingles and glass windows and roared down the metal gutters in a raging torrent.

It should have been a horrible night, a night of depression, drunkenness, and nightmare, but she was there and he was able to survive. When he shivered in bed, she nestled her body close to his, her sweet breath warming his face. When he lapsed into nightmare, she shook him with gentle hands, not quite waking, just prodding, hard enough to drive off the demons. And that night, for the first time in what seemed his entire adult life, he slept straight through until morning.

Fourteen

Dorothy called the next morning while Carpo was having coffee on the porch with Amanda and Floyd. She called from the library to say that a librarian in Southbury had come across an expired library card for a T. Donovan. With no better ideas on how to locate Trent Donovan, Carpo kissed Amanda good-bye, hopped in the rental car, and drove to Southbury, a midsize town about twenty miles east of Bridgewater.

The Southbury Public Library sat on the town's main strip: a four-lane road with classic New England–style architecture sandwiched between fast food joints and modern concrete eyesores. The library was one of the eyesores, a fiery red building with tinted windows and an overbearing design that would have been suited better as a bomb shelter.

Carpo walked straight to the reference desk and asked for Nathaniel Darvey, as Dorothy had instructed him to do. Darvey was a spry little man, somewhere in his sixties, with standard-issue librarian glasses dangling from his neck. The man's voice matched his stature, low and soft, and he had a bad habit of swallowing in the middle of his sentences. Carpo found that he had to stare at the man's lips in order to decipher what he was saying.

After a brief introduction Darvey led Carpo to a cluttered office behind the circulation desk. Carpo took a seat as Darvey, whistling a faint rendition of "Moon River," thumbed through the contents of a six-drawer filing cabinet. After a few minutes he plucked a green index card from the cabinet and waved it in the air.

"Here he is," he said, swallowing excitedly. "T. Donovan. Owes us five books. Checked them out August of 'ninety-two, and that's the last we heard of him." Darvey stepped behind the desk, punched the keys on a calculator. "That's $16.53 in late dues. And if he *lost* the books, it'll run him"—Darvey punched more keys—"$63.42. They were hard-cover," he explained.

Carpo smiled to show that he appreciated the man's quick calculations. "Is there an address on the card?" he asked.

Darvey checked the card; a troubled expression weighed on his thin eyebrows. "No, just a phone number."

"I assume you've called it and nobody by that name lives there anymore?"

"No, he's there," Darvey said. "I've talked to him several times."

"You've talked to him?"

"Yes." He pointed at the card. "Look, I wrote down the dates. The last time I called was April twenty-ninth. He just refuses to come in and pay the late charges."

Carpo rose from his chair, peered over Darvey's shoulder. "Do you know what the T stands for?"

"Dorothy asked the same thing. I don't know."

"Would you mind if I called him now?"

Darvey pointed at the telephone next to the calculator. Carpo took the library card, made a mental note of the number, then dialed it. He let it ring twenty times, but no one answered.

"Do you think he's moved?" Darvey asked after Carpo had put down the telephone.

"I don't know. Does the library keep a set of Cole's Directories? You know, reverse phone books?"

Darvey nodded, then led Carpo back to the reference desk. He pointed at a shelf holding the familiar thick green phone books that enable a person to look up the resident and address for a particular phone number. Carpo pulled out the directory for Southbury and flipped to the page that held the same number as the library card. It was listed to G. Kingston, 221 Summers Street.

Darvey clucked his tongue, upset that the number hadn't panned out. Carpo flipped to the front of the directory to check the publication date. The book was three years old, meaning that the T. Donovan on the library card might have moved to Summers Street after the book was published. It was also possible that he had changed his name to G. Kingston, or he might have lied about his telephone number on the library card. But that still didn't explain Darvey's assertion that he had spoken to the man. Carpo decided the only way to settle the matter was to drive to 221 Summers Street and see who, if anyone, answered a knock on the door.

Darvey gave clear directions to Summers Street, except that Carpo missed one street because the librarian had swallowed while saying the name. He backtracked and found the correct street, which connected a few blocks later to Summers Street. Number 221 was a spacious Tudor stone mansion set at the midpoint of a semicircle cobblestone driveway. A freshly waxed Jaguar convertible was parked by the front door.

At the sight of the car, Carpo felt quite confident that Trent Donovan no longer lived here; what person with a Jaguar couldn't afford $16.53 in late-book fees? But he parked anyway, walked to the door, and rang the bell. A series of bells chimed deep within the house, and a minute later a woman answered the door. She looked to be in her mid-forties, thin, and very pretty, wearing skintight riding britches and knee-high riding boots.

"Good afternoon," Carpo announced in a voice that he imagined as official sounding. "My name is Nathaniel Darvey. I'm the circulations manager at Southbury Public Library. Does a Trent Donovan live here?"

The question seemed to fluster the woman. She brushed an imaginary strand of hair off her face. "Yes, he lives here. Is he in trouble for something?"

"Mr. Donovan has five books from the library that are overdue. He owes $16.53 in late fees, and if they're lost or damaged, he'll have to pay for their replacement."

"He does?" The woman's face relaxed, a queer smile creeping over it. "Hang on, I'll get him."

Carpo waited on the stoop for the woman's return, thinking that something felt wrong about the situation. Firstly, none of the other members of Justice for Southville had been wealthy; not even Jack, who had been the most famous member of the group. Secondly, the woman was too young to be Trent Donovan's wife or girlfriend. Still, he knew from his job that he shouldn't take anything at face value. Perhaps Trent Donovan had done well since moving from Bridgewater. Perhaps so well, he had found a new mate.

The door opened and the woman reappeared. Standing at her side was a boy, twelve or thirteen years old, wearing a T-shirt from a Pearl Jam concert.

The woman motioned toward Carpo, saying to the boy: "This is the man who came to see you, Trent."

"Trent Donovan?" Carpo asked weakly.

The boy looked between the woman and Carpo, then nodded.

"You have some overdue books," Carpo mumbled. "You'll have to return them and pay the late fees before you can check any more books out of the library."

A wise-ass scowl came over the kid's face. "What are you? The library police?"

"Trent, don't be rude," the woman said. "Mr.—umm . . . what did you say your name was?"

"Car—" Carpo started to say, then caught himself, "Darvey. Nathaniel Darvey."

"Yes, Mr. Darvey, could I return the books now and give you money for the late charges?"

Not wanting to cart an armful of books back to the library, Carpo shook his head. "Unfortunately, I'm not authorized to make collections."

The kid rolled his eyes and disappeared inside the house. The woman smiled apologetically for his behavior. She promised to return the books that afternoon and thanked him for stopping by. As she closed the door, Carpo said: "Ma'am, can I ask one more question?"

The door stopped, halfway closed. "Yes?"

"Do you know any other Donovans in the area? I'm trying to locate a man by the same name from the Bridgewater system."

"More overdue books?"

"Something like that."

"I don't know any other Donovans in Southbury, but I hear there's a few in Roxbury."

"What about Bridgewater? Know any from there?"

She shook her head. "I don't."

The woman was beginning to sound irked, but Carpo persisted. "Is Trent your son?"

"Yes."

The door started to close; Carpo stepped closer. "Then why is his last name different from the name of the owner of the house?"

"Because I remarried!" The woman frowned so hard, her eyebrows touched. "What's with these questions?" she demanded. "You really are like the library police!"

Without waiting for a response, she slammed the door in his face.

Carpo called Dorothy from a pay phone in the parking lot of a Dairy Queen. He related the episode with Trent Donovan, the twelve-year-old wise-ass from Southbury— the *wrong* Trent Donovan. Dorothy, hearing the irritation in his voice, took some time explaining her theory.

"I don't know how else to do it, I've tried every other method for finding people. I checked the state directories, voting records, tax assessments, liens, and I ran a search in the local papers. Checking library cards is the only way I know that will get us names."

"But we must be forgetting something," Carpo said, trying to think of other resources available to the public.

"Sure, there's others. Mortgages, voter registration, auto

registration, even speeding tickets, but we don't have a month to wait for the paperwork to clear."

"Paperwork?"

"Aren't you a journalist?" Dorothy snapped. "Some of those require access through the Freedom of Information Act."

"Right," Carpo said, even though he couldn't recall which *did* require an FOIA filing. "Listen, Dorothy, you're obviously the pro here, just tell me how I can help."

"Well"—Carpo could hear the sound of paper crinkling— "I've found Donovans listed at the libraries in Roxbury, Brookfield, Kent, and Torrington. I think we should check each one."

"Torrington?" Carpo groaned. "That's an hour's drive from here. It's going to take days to check all those places, and that's assuming that Trent Donovan even *goes* to the library. Can't we narrow the list?"

"I don't think so," she said, "besides having the librarians . . ."

"What?"

"Well, I could have them check what each of these Donovans is reading. The type of books. It might give us an idea about the type of person he is."

Carpo squinted, unsure of the idea. "You think we can put together a profile of a person just by the books they read?"

"We do it all the time here."

"And are you accurate?"

"I may not be able to predict the color of the car they drive, but I can tell you if it's foreign or domestic."

He ran his fingers through his hair. "It sounds so . . . unscientific."

"Then you'll just have to visit every Donovan on this list."

She has a point, he thought. "Tell me how it would work."

"Let's say, for example, our T. Donovan is checking out titles like *Green Eggs and Ham* or *Our Bodies, Our Selves.* We'll know immediately it's not the right person."

"Unless he's checking them out for his kids or his wife. Dorothy, this doesn't sound foolproof."

"What is foolproof?" she asked testily. "I know you're eager to find Trent Donovan. I am too, but unless you can think up something better, I don't think you should complain."

He didn't have a better idea. In fact, he didn't have a worse one. He couldn't think of a single other option.

"Okay, let's do it," he said. "Get on the horn and ask your librarian friends what all the T. Donovans in the county are reading. And start with Roxbury. I'm only twenty minutes away, so I'll head there first. When I'm done, I'll call you for the rest."

"Speak to you, then," Dorothy said before they hung up.

Of all the libraries Carpo had visited, the Roxbury Public Library best mirrored its residents: new, modern, and wealthy. Out front, a large bronze plaque listed the names of the people who had donated money for the branch's recent construction; several, Carpo noted, belonged to well-known authors, including Jack Crawford. Inside, the library smelled plastic and clean, like a car just off the dealer's lot. And most surprising of all, the librarian at the reference desk was under sixty-five; Carpo had been starting to wonder if library jobs were filled according to the number of one's gray hairs. Phil Kaplan debunked that theory. He was in his mid-thirties, with brown hair tied in a ponytail. Not a strand of gray in sight.

"I got off the phone with Dorothy ten minutes ago," he said after Carpo introduced himself. "Let me grab the cards."

He returned with a stack of library cards the same shape and color as the cards at the Southbury library.

"Dorothy didn't say how far back I should look, so I pulled every Donovan we had." He fanned seven cards across the deck. "Royal flush," he said.

"That seems like a lot of T. Donovans," Carpo said. "How large is Roxbury?"

"We're not very big, but we've kept good files over the years. Some of these cards go back to the fifties."

"But *seven* of them?"

The librarian shrugged. "Maybe they're related."

Carpo flipped through the cards, interested only in the ones that dated after 1990. Two matched that criterion. He scribbled the information in his notebook, thankful that the cards listed both street addresses and telephone numbers. One of the T. Donovans lived on South Street, the other on Main Street. It wouldn't take long to drive to either location, but he decided to put Dorothy's theory to the test.

"Is there any way we can look up the titles of the books these two checked out?" he asked. "I want to see if it's possible to rule one of them out."

The librarian frowned. "How?"

"Dorothy thinks it might be possible to determine the person by what they're reading."

"Like a man would likely be the one reading *Popular Mechanics?*"

Carpo shrugged. "Pretty crazy idea, huh?"

The librarian tapped his index finger on his forehead. "Actually, it's an interesting one. I think it could even work, provided they're steady readers."

"So you can do it?"

"No, unfortunately it won't work here. Because of the construction, we didn't go online until two years after everybody else. All these cards are listed by date. You'd have to leaf through each day's log, find the correct name, trace the ISBN number, then match it to the title. It'd be a lot of work."

Carpo thought he understood the explanation, and in any case, it sounded complicated enough that he didn't want to try it. He thanked the librarian for his help, then went to the pay phone. He dropped a quarter in the slot and called the first T. Donovan, the one who lived on South Street. The man who answered said his name was Ted, and that he had lived all his life in Roxbury. The second T. Donovan was even farther off the mark. The T stood for Tricia, and she described herself to Carpo like a personals ad: "I'm forty-six years old, with no husband, no kids, and no pets." Worst of all, neither Ted nor Tricia had ever known a Trent.

He dialed the New Milford library and got put on hold at the research desk. He followed the progress of a clock's second hand, his spirits and energy barely keeping pace. Just when he started wondering if they had forgotten about him, Dorothy came on the line.

"Splendid news, dear!" she said. "I just got off the phone with Mona Carter, the librarian from the Brookfield branch.

It seems she has a T. Donovan who reads some very interesting books."

He rolled his eyes, but checked his tongue.

"Last month this person checked out *The Ultimate Guide to Baseball* and *The Summer of '42.*"

"I get it," he said sarcastically. "Baseball is a guy sport, so obviously this T. Donovan is a man. Sorry, Dorothy, but I know a lot of women who follow baseball."

"I'm one of them," she said, "but this Donovan also checked out a retirement planner and a manual on setting up a living will."

"So?"

"So, it's an age indicator. It means he's probably old enough to be thinking about retiring or dying."

"Is that all we have to go on? Baseball memoirs and legal advice? I wish there were more."

"There is, dear, I've saved the best for last. Our friend T. Donovan also checked out two books, both nonfiction: *An African American in Paris* and *Son of a Gunsmith*. Don't those sound familiar?"

Carpo felt his skin tingle. *Dorothy is right,* he realized, *it must be the real Trent Donovan. Both books were written by Jack.*

Humbled, he asked: "Dorothy, did your friend Mona happen to have an address for this particular Donovan?"

Fifteen

The address Dorothy recited was unfamiliar to Carpo: 1170 Obtuse Rocks Road. He looked it up in the library's road atlas when he got off the telephone. The street was located on the outskirts of Brookfield, just a quarter-mile past the Lillinonah bridge and almost directly parallel to Jack's cottage. If this Trent Donovan was the correct Trent Donovan, then he and Jack practically could have waved to each other across the valley.

He set off for Brookfield, stomach gnawing at his insides; it was two o'clock in the afternoon and he hadn't had anything to eat since breakfast. This time he ignored the urge to stop for something. He didn't want another lunch break to cost someone their life.

Despite its name, when he reached Obtuse Rocks Road there wasn't a rock or boulder in sight, nor anything that looked obtuse. The road dipped and curved through a forest of pine trees with thick fanlike branches, that blotted out the sun and littered the ground with aromatic needles. A mile down the road he spotted a stone marker with the numbers 1170 painted on it and turned in.

The driveway was steep, with a coarse gravel surface that gurgled like ocean surf as the tires ran through it. He drove higher and higher, up to where the pine forest started to thin. A faint logging trail wound through the trees on the right, and at the top the driveway ended at a wood cabin. It was about as big as Jack's cottage and faced the lake, its sides stained dark green from the recent rain.

He parked next to a two-door Toyota. The car had blue license plates painted with a small wheelchair, denoting handicapped. He also noticed the plywood board that covered the front steps, creating a ramp to the door. He walked to the door and knocked. Two minutes passed before he knocked again, louder. After another wait he raised his fist, preparing to give the door a real pounding, when he heard a metallic creak from the other side. A moment later a stern voice demanded: "Who is it?"

"My name is Michael Carpo. I'm a journalist from New York City. I'm looking for Trent Donovan."

"You've got the wrong address."

He stared at the door, wishing he could see through it. The marker at the bottom of the driveway had said 1170, and Dorothy had repeated the number three times; he did not have the wrong address. "I must speak to you, Mr. Donovan. You're in grave danger."

"I'll pass the warning along if I ever meet him. Have a good day."

The metallic squeak came through the door, followed by a groan as human weight shifted. Another creak, another groan. Trent Donovan was walking away.

"Mr. Donovan, I'm a friend of Jack Crawford's. I watch his cottage every summer. I don't know if you've heard, sir, but Jack died Sunday. They say he committed suicide, but I know it was a murder."

The metallic squeaks stopped.

"Then Elizabeth Jessup drowned at the marina," he continued, "that was on Tuesday, and just yesterday I found Fern Gimlins's body at his house. Mr. Donovan, I know why you're all dying. It's because of your group, Justice for Southville. Please, let me help you."

The metallic creaks started again, this time, toward the door. Locks clicked, then the door opened, the security chain still fastened. Trent Donovan poked his face into the space. He must have been around Jack's age, mid-seventies, though he looked much older, bent over an aluminum walker as if his back were broken. Deep wrinkles etched his forehead, eyes, and the corners of his mouth, indicating a life lived before sunscreen. The few hairs remaining on his head had turned gray.

But in his eyes there was plenty of life. Clear blue, they flashed from the shadows like buried embers, measuring him up. "Fern's dead?"

"Yes, sir. He was murdered yesterday afternoon."

"What happened to him?"

Carpo shook his head. "It was terrible. They didn't even try to make it look like suicide."

"I asked what happened to him."

He winced. "They cut his throat."

Trent nodded, face emotionless, as if to show the news didn't surprise him. "That all you came to say?"

"No, sir. I came to help you."

Trent scowled. "Son, how do you think you're going to help me?"

The question caught him unprepared. "I could get you some police protection or something."

"I tried calling the cops two years ago, back when this all started. I'm still waiting for them to show up." He stepped back from the door. "If you'd really like to help, stay away. The last thing I need is traffic on the road showing the world I'm up here."

"But, Mr. Donovan, you can't hide forever."

"I don't intend to. Just till Monday."

"What's Monday?"

Trent broke into a smile. "Guess you don't know as much as you think."

"I never claimed to," Carpo said, irked. "But I still think I can help."

"How did you find me, son?"

"A librarian from New Milford checked the various local branches for any library cards made out to T. Donovan." Carpo shrugged. "I guess we got lucky that you're a reader."

"I didn't even know they kept records of that," Trent muttered. "How utterly careless."

The old man moved away from the door and slammed it. Carpo stared at the handle a few seconds, shocked. The conversation had felt bad from the start; he cursed himself for not preparing something better to say. He turned and started down the ramp, when he heard the chain drag across its slide. The door opened again and Trent Donovan stood before him in full view.

"Come back, son. I don't mean to be so rude, but I got to watch who I trust these days. Let's go inside and talk there, I need to sit. My hip is aching something fierce."

He shuffled into the house, hands squeezing the foam handles of the walker so hard, the bones showed through his knuckles. Carpo fell in behind him, taking one step for every five of his.

"Busted my hip last winter," Trent explained, out of breath. "Taken me a lifetime to heal. Go ahead and wait in the living room. I'll be along in a bit."

Carpo squeezed past the man and walked to the living room, a large bright space with a high ceiling, exposed rafters, and authentic log walls. The room was barren, the only objects being a small couch, a reclining chair, and a small table. Wide spaces separated the furniture, so, Carpo imagined, Trent could maneuver with his walker. Like the cottage, a bay window overlooked the lake, next to a door that opened onto a brick patio. Carpo looked across the valley. Through the trees he could make out the roof and chimney of Jack's cottage.

A stack of books sat on the table; Carpo checked the titles to see if he recognized them. All but two were the ones Dorothy had named on the phone; her reading-card theory had worked to perfection. When Trent appeared, he squeaked to the reclining chair, planted his hands on the armrests, and lowered himself into the seat.

"Pretty view here," Carpo remarked, filling the dead space while Trent caught his breath. "It's almost the same as Jack's, except from the other direction."

Trent ignored the comment. He grabbed a corncob pipe off the table, then twisted his body left and pulled a leather pouch out of his back pocket. He unrolled it and began to stuff clumps of brown, black, and orange tobacco into the bowl. "Were you the one who found Jack?" he asked when he had finished filling the pipe.

Carpo nodded. "I found him when I arrived the first day.

He was in the bathroom with the door closed. His dog, Floyd, was in there too."

"You find Bethie Jessup too?"

"No, sir, she drowned in the lake in the middle of the night. A neighbor heard her dogs barking, went down to the marina, and found her."

"And what about Fern? How did you find him?"

"I looked his address up in the phone book and drove over there yesterday afternoon. Like I said, his throat was cut when I got there. It's the first death that doesn't look like an accident or suicide. I think the killers are starting to panic."

Trent didn't say anything, unzipping a pocket on the side of the tobacco pouch to pull out a book of paper matches. He ripped one off and dragged it across the sulfur strip, then waved the flame over the top of the bowl. His cheeks worked furiously as he sucked in the smoke, puffing until a bright orange glow emanated from the center of the bowl and a cloud of vanilla-scented smoke pillowed his head. "Why do you keep using the plural?" he asked. "Are you telling me there's more than one killer?"

"Fern Gimlins was still alive when I got there. He managed to say that he recognized the people who killed him."

"Did he mention names?"

"No, sir. His throat was so mangled, I could barely make out what he was whispering."

"And what was that?"

" 'I know them.' That's what he was saying, over and over: 'I know them, I know them.' "

"That is news," Trent mumbled, pipe clenched tightly between his teeth. As he spoke, wisps of smoke escaped his lips, punctuating each syllable. "We always figured it was someone close to us, otherwise people wouldn't have let down their guard. But I never thought about there being more than one person."

"Why?"

"Greed, mostly." Trent shrugged. "I figured the person would want to keep all that money for himself." He looked at Carpo. "You know what money I'm referring to?"

"I'm not sure. I presume it's from the court ruling thirty years ago, when your group was named owner of the land below the lake."

"You've done some homework."

"Yes, but you said Monday was significant. What happens that day?"

"Justice for Southville takes full legal control of the lake. As owners, we'll be able to negotiate a new lease agreement with the state."

Trent plucked the pipe from his lips, studied the inside of the bowl. Carpo watched with a mixture of horror and fascination as he stuck his thumb into the bowl, tamping down the tobacco ash. Carpo didn't know how he could withstand the intense heat inside the bowl, until Trent pulled out his thumb. It had a scar on the tip as black as charred wood.

"Mr. Donovan, why did it take so long for Justice for Southville to realize that its members were being murdered?"

"We did," he said quietly. "We noticed. Fact, we even had a meeting over at Jack's place two years ago. Frank Washington had died in a freak accident and Jack kept insisting more than just fate was causing all these bad things to happen."

"He died of beestings, right?"

"Yep, he was mowing the lawn and his tractor ran over a hornet's nest. I don't know, I still say it was an accident, but he was the third to die that year and we were all getting jumpy, waiting to see who would be next. Some people bought watchdogs, some installed burglar alarms, some bought guns. Didn't matter none. One after the next, we kept dying."

"Is that when you decided to leave Bridgewater?"

"Guns aren't my style, I figured I'd just end up shooting myself. And I'm allergic to dogs. So I did the only thing that I knew would preserve me. I disappeared."

"And the police really wouldn't help?"

Trent snorted, producing a gurgle in the pipe bowl. "You mean Trooper Walker? He's police around here, and he practically laughed us out of town."

"Why did so many members remain in Bridgewater?"

"Where were we supposed to go? This was home to us, it's where we were born and married, it's where we raised our children. It takes a lot to make a man move from a place like that. Even if the price for staying means death."

Trent looked out the bay window to where the sun was dipping on the far side of the valley, over Lake Lillinonah. "For years I used to look at that lake and hate it. I used to call it 'the dam' because to me that's what it was: a goddamn shame.

"But having that lake also motivated our group. It reminded us of what had been taken, and kept us united. It made us strong. Strong enough to beat the state at its own game. They used their laws to take our homes and we used those same laws to win something back. We hauled them into the same courthouses and hired the same slick Hartford lawyers. Now, when I look down at that lake, I see it as a miracle, the most incredible, beautiful lake in the world."

Trent closed his eyes and laughed, his upper lip curling high on the pipe stem. His pride was infectious, and Carpo smiled with him.

"Does anybody know you moved here?" Carpo asked.

The smile was still on Trent's face, but it seemed to have frozen. Suddenly, a dark shadow fell over his face. His chest started heaving and he grabbed at his throat as if he were choking.

"Mr. Donovan, you okay?"

He hacked loudly into his fist for several seconds, then his throat cleared. "Damn pipe cuts my wind," he explained between gasps. He pulled a handkerchief from his pocket and mopped his forehead. When his normal breathing had returned, he straightened his body, plopped the pipe back into his mouth, and relit it. "Now, where were we?" he asked.

"I asked if anybody knew you moved here."

"Only Jack. I told him in case there was an emergency. He was like a brother to me, and I trusted him with the information."

"You didn't trust the others?"

"I did. Least, most of them. But the way they were dropping, I didn't trust anybody too much. Money does bad things to people. I've seen it destroy many good people, so I can imagine what it does to the rotten ones." He coughed once more into his fist. "Besides, I think all the anticipation about the lease money is the reason we didn't watch out for each other better."

"What do you mean?"

"Simple mathematics, son. If someone died, it meant a bigger piece of the pie for everyone else."

Carpo frowned, shocked. "The piece doesn't get passed to the relatives of the deceased?"

"Not the way Jack had the lease drawn up. He made it so only the original members of the group could draw on the first renewal. It was supposed to protect us from having a deceased member's family tie up all the money in court. In the end, that's probably what is killing us. The money doesn't transfer until the next generation, when all the original members are dead."

"And how much money are we talking about?"

Trent's blue eyes narrowed. "Can't say really. We was supposed to start negotiating Monday. If I make it to then, I expect there'll be about a million dollars at stake."

"How do you figure that?"

"Jack came up with a scheme for deciding how much we'd rent the lake to the state for. He looked up what C.L.& P. takes in every year in power charges, about ten million dollars, and then decided we deserved a ten-percent fee from that, annually."

"How did he come up with that?"

Trent smiled. "He said that was what his agent charged for negotiating all of his manuscripts. He figured it was as good a way as any for negotiating this contract too."

"So Monday's the day," Carpo said. "It must be why three people have died this week."

"Can't think of a better explanation for it."

"Is it possible that a relative of one of the deceased members is doing this? Maybe trying to knock off all the members so the money will get passed to the next generation?"

"I suppose anything is possible, but it'd be awfully stupid. A couple of hundred people would draw on that money, what with all the children and grandchildren floating around. Their take would amount to five or ten grand at best."

"That still sounds like a nice chunk of change, Mr. Donovan."

"Naw, not really. Not enough to murder so many people for. Besides, if what Fern told you is true, I don't like to believe that there's more than one rotten apple in our families."

"Who else, then? Who else would want you all dead?"

"Son, we've been racking our brains for two years about that. I figure I'll either find out over the weekend, or else I'll make it to Monday and it'll be too late for them to touch me."

"If I have any say, you'll make it to Monday just fine."

Trent chuckled, then brought the pipe back to his lips. "I wish I felt as confident as you sound, son. I got a feeling in my gut this is going to be a hell of a long weekend."

Sixteen

There was a feeling in Carpo's gut too, a mixture of relief and anxiety, as he backed down the driveway and started for Bridgewater. One burden had been lifted from his shoulders—he had found Trent Donovan alive—but another burden had been dumped firmly in its place. Now he had to make sure Trent stayed alive another three days. He wasn't too cocky to acknowledge that if he and Dorothy could find Trent within a day, so could someone else.

So where does one hide a seventy-three-year-old handicapped man?

Carpo addressed that question before he left the cabin, asking Mr. Donovan if he'd consider moving to Jack's cottage for the weekend so he could watch him. Trent would hear nothing of it.

"I've lived here for two years without a single uninvited car coming up that driveway until yours did this afternoon. Should I abandon ship because of one minor incident?" He shook his head vigorously. "No, I'm safer here than I'd ever be in Bridgewater. That's where all the murders happened. I'm not going."

As Carpo drove to Bridgewater, alone, he tried to rationalize the decision. Trent Donovan *had* survived more than two years there and, if there was a problem, he could still reach the cabin within five minutes. Plus, they had one other advantage: the Brookfield Public Library was closed on weekends.

The sun had started to dip behind Trent's side of the valley by the time he parked outside the cottage; the trees projected narrow black shadows across the driveway, like rows of iron bars. In a sense, the cottage had become his prison cell. He was on twenty-four-hour call for the weekend, and that meant he couldn't stray far. It was not how he'd planned to spend his final weekend in the country, though nothing had happened as planned this vacation.

Floyd was in extra hyper spirits when he unlocked the cottage. After two days pent up indoors, the dog looked like he could use a good run, so Carpo took him to the backyard.

Once, Jack had claimed that Floyd came from the pedigree of field trial champions. Carpo supposed it was true, though by the way the dog played fetch, it didn't appear as though many of the prize dog genes had come down to him. Floyd's idea of fetch was keep away: careening around the yard, dodging any move of Carpo's. And if Carpo didn't give chase, Floyd would plop down on the lawn and chew the stick. During one of these wild pursuits, Carpo heard the telephone ring. He pounced on the dog, wrestled away the stick, and ran for the cottage, reaching the phone on its twelfth ring. "Hello?"

"Carpo, it's me. Where've you been?"

It was Amanda, her tone noticeably cold. "Gosh, I'm sorry," he said. "I've been out looking for Trent Donovan all afternoon. I just got back."

"How did it go?"

He started to answer, then stopped. Last night he had told her about the murders: that Jack's suicide seemed linked to Elizabeth Jessup's accident and a few of the other, unexplained deaths in town. That morning, after Dorothy had called, he had also told her why he needed to find Trent Donovan. Now he wished he hadn't said anything. At least, not until Monday. "Yes, I found him."

"Terrific. Where was he?"

He hesitated again. It was one thing to say that he had found Trent, quite another to say where. He decided the best response would be no answer at all. "He's great. He's alive and safe. I think it's going to work out fine."

"Great, but where did you find him?"

"I checked just about every town in Litchfield County, it turns out he was right near here. You wouldn't believe the number of places I checked."

"He was in Bridgewater the whole time?"

"Not quite."

She matched his silence for a moment, then laughed. "Okay, okay, I get the hint. You want to keep it secret."

He laughed too, embarrassed. "It's not that I don't trust you, I just wa—"

"Carpo, you don't have to explain. I'm just glad you found him. It's not even why I'm calling. Tonight is the opening of the Bridgewater Fair. I'm wondering if you'd like to be my date?"

"I can't," he said, grimacing. "I promised Mr. Donovan I would stay near the phone in case he needs me."

"Bummer, Carpo, I was hoping we could go. It's kind of corny but really good fun."

"I've always wanted to go, but I just can't leave the

cottage. I'd feel terrible if something happened to Mr. Donovan while I was gone." Suddenly, he got an idea. "Say, why
don't you come over here instead? I could cook us dinner.
In fact, I'll even make Jack's famous dish: eight-by-eight
marinated pork chops."

"That sounds great. What can I bring?"

"Just yourself." His sour mood lifted at the thought of
seeing her. "Come on over whenever you can."

"I'll be there in an hour or so."

After hanging up the telephone, he went to the freezer
and removed the packet of pork chops that Jack always kept
on hand. He put the chops in the sink and ran hot water
over them to defrost them. Then he concocted the marinade.

Jack used to insist on marinating his chops for eight
hours. Carpo figured they would eat dinner around ten, in
just three hours, so to make up for the lost time he made
the mixture extra strong. In a deep bowl he combined two
cups of soy sauce, one cup of honey, and one diced garlic
bulb. He mixed the elements with a fork, until the soy sauce
accepted the honey, and the black, oily brew was steeped
with garlic, then he added the chops. He covered the bowl
with plastic wrap and set it on top of the refrigerator, out
of Floyd's reach. Next, he headed to the garden for salad
ingredients.

Humid nights, cool mornings, and the recent rainstorm
had sparked a growth explosion in the garden: weeds, slugs,
beetles and very big vegetables. It didn't help that he had
neglected to weed or tie up the tomato plants all week. He
waded into the jungle, bare feet clinging to the moist topsoil,
and picked three beefsteak tomatoes, a cucumber, and an
assortment of red, green, and yellow peppers. He walked

along the exterior of the fence, where the berry bushes were planted, and picked a mixed pint of raspberries and blueberries. He didn't have the time or ingredients on hand to bake a pie for dessert, but he knew the berries would taste just fine with a little cream and sugar sprinkled on the top.

Back inside, he washed and shredded a head of lettuce and put it in a large wooden bowl. He chopped the tomatoes, diced the peppers, added a sweet Vidalia onion and salt and pepper. All he had left to do was mix a vinaigrette salad dressing, throw the pork chops on the grill, and dinner would be ready.

He tuned the radio to a local classic rock station, went into the bathroom, and shaved and showered. As he toweled the water off his body, he noticed Floyd lying in his usual position: near, but not touching, the entrance to the bathroom.

"Come on, boy," he coaxed, slapping his knee. "Here you go, Floydie. Come here."

The dog groaned and rolled onto his back, but his nose didn't move any closer to the threshold.

Feeling frisky over the approaching dinner date, he dressed in a pair of khaki shorts and a wild Madras shirt that he had bought on Canal Street in New York City. The shirt had a fluorescent palm-tree pattern on the front and back; he wore it with the top three buttons undone. He slapped some of Jack's Aqua Velva aftershave on his cheeks and combed his hair back, the wetness turning it black and shiny. He went to the living room and dialed Trent's number from memory. The phone rang twenty times before Trent answered, breathless.

"Mr. Donovan, it's me, Carpo. Are you okay?"

"I was okay," Trent snapped, "until I had to drag my hip across the room to get the damn telephone."

"I'm sorry, I was just making sure that everything's going well. Do you need anything?"

"I'm perfectly fine. Everything I need is right at my side . . . except the telephone."

He smiled at the man's gruff tone, something about it reminding him of Jack. "Don't forget that I'm here," he said. "If you need anything, even groceries or a newspaper, just call."

"I won't forget."

After hanging up, he thought of Dorothy. He still hadn't called her back since that afternoon; she didn't even know he had found Trent Donovan. Since there was little chance she was still at the library, he called information for New Milford and got her home number. A man—Carpo assumed it was her husband—answered the telephone.

"Hi," Carpo said, "may I please speak to Dorothy?"

"Who's calling?"

"It's Michael Carpo."

"Aah, the mysterious Michael Carpo," the man said in a way that did not sound friendly. "Dorothy's talked of little else this week. She's still at the library."

"She's still there?"

"Yes, awaiting your call."

He thanked the man, reestablished a dial tone, and called the library. Dorothy answered immediately. "Hello?"

"It's Carpo."

"Where the heck have you been?"

"I'm sorry, I should have called sooner, but I forgot. I just got home a little while ago."

"Don't you check your answering machine?"

From where he was standing, he could see the red light flashing on the unit, signaling several messages on the tape. "I didn't think of it," he said. "As soon as I got back from Trent Donovan's house, I took Floyd outside for some exercise."

"What do you mean by that?"

Carpo frowned. "Floyd's been cooped up all day and I thou—"

"Not about that," she interrupted, "what do you mean by Trent Donovan?"

"I found him. Your idea worked perfectly."

"You found Trent Donovan? It must be the wrong person. He's in Bridgewater. This morning he turned himself in to the state trooper and asked for protection. He's going to spend the weekend there."

"What are you talking about?" He squeezed the phone. "Trent Donovan is at Trooper Walker's house?"

"Yes, he's been there all day. I would have told you sooner if I could have reached you."

"But, Dorothy, it's not possible. I just got off the telephone with him five minutes ago. He's in Brookfield. I called him at his home."

"Well, now he's over at Trooper Walker's. My friend, Clara, whom I play bridge with on Tuesday nights, heard it from her husband, who happens to be a friend of Trooper Walker's brother-in-law. Anyway, Clara says Trent Donovan is asking for police protection until Monday morning. For the past two years he's been hiding in Lyme, Connecticut."

Dorothy was silent for a moment, then said, "What I'm saying, Carpo, is that he's safe. Trent Donovan is still alive."

"Dorothy, I swear, I got off the phone with him no more than five minutes ago."

"Maybe he didn't mention where he was."

"I dialed the number in Brookfield. I also spent two hours with him this afternoon. He has no intention of turning himself over to Trooper Walker. I couldn't even get him to come with me."

The silence on the line indicated that she finally understood what he had said. He could imagine her magnified eyelids batting up and down, as if beating back the shock.

"I know it's late, Dorothy, but I need a favor. Can you meet me at Trooper Walker's house?"

"What time?"

"As soon as possible."

"Sure, Carpo, whatever you say."

"And I need you to bring that photograph along, the one you showed me at the library yesterday, with all the members of Justice for Southville."

"Where does Trooper Walker live?"

"He's in the center of Bridgewater, directly across from the Village Store. In fact, park in the Village Store parking lot. No one will be using it at this hour. We'll meet there."

"I'm on my way."

"And, Dorothy," he said, "don't mention this to anyone. At least, not until we know which Trent Donovan is the real one."

Seventeen

When Amanda arrived a few minutes later, Carpo didn't wait for her to come inside. He walked to the driveway and stood by the driver-side door, car keys in hand.

"What's the matter?" she asked after she'd gotten out.

"A man turned up at Trooper Walker's house today seeking protection until Monday. He claims to be Trent Donovan. I don't know if he is or not, but he certainly isn't the same man I found this afternoon."

"Who do you think it is?"

"I don't know. I'm going over to Trooper Walker's house right now to find out."

"I'll go with you. I'll drive."

"No, Amanda, if you don't mind, I'd like you to stay here. I told Trent Donovan, the one I met earlier, that he could call me if anything goes wrong. I need you to be here in case he calls. Could you do that for me?"

"Sure, no problem."

"The pork chops are marinating on top of the fridge. Don't let Floyd near them, or he'll eat them. If you get hungry, throw them on the grill for eight minutes a side. And there's plenty of wine in the—"

"Carpo, don't worry about me, I'll be fine. I'll wait until you get back and then we'll have dinner together."

"I don't know how long I'll be. It could take a couple of hours."

"Not to worry. I'll hang out with Floyd and sip some vino." She held up a paperback novel. "Look, I even brought a book."

They walked to the other side of the driveway, her arm looped through his, to where the rental car was parked. He opened the door, slid behind the steering wheel, and put the key in the ignition.

"Carpo, wait a sec."

He looked up, hand on the key. "What's the matter?"

"Be careful," she said, then blushed. "I know that sounds silly, I mean, we've known each other only a week, but I don't want anything bad to happen."

He twisted the key, and the car came to life. "Nothing bad will happen," he said over the engine's weak sputter. "I promise."

As he reached for the door, Amanda leaned inside. She took his face in her hands, tilted up his chin, and planted a heavyweight kiss on his mouth. His eyes ballooned, a wave of gender confusion sweeping him. No woman had ever taken the kissing initiative with him so directly. But it felt right: tender, with a sense of urgency. He wished it could have lasted all night.

She stepped back and slammed the door. He reversed the car as he rolled down the window. "Keep that bottle of wine on ice," he called to her. "I'll try to wrap this up quickly."

She responded with a wave, then placed her hands

together, as if making a prayer. As he drove off, he watched her in the rearview mirror: blond hair billowing in the wind; loose-skirted dress hugging tightly to the rest of her.

All this heady, romantic interplay ended up costing Carpo some valuable time. He was thinking about that kiss, the way she had delivered it, and how much he wanted to get back to the cottage to try it again. What he should have been thinking about was the fastest way to get to Trooper Walker's house.

He hit traffic on Route 7 from the Bridgewater Fair while still three miles from the town center. Hundreds of cars lined both sides of the road. Every house on the street had its front yard roped off, the owners collecting twenty dollars a car for parking. Those three miles ended up taking forty minutes to cover. Forty full minutes of fiddling with the radio, slapping the air bag, stop and go, wall to wall, rush-hour-in-Manhattan type of congestion.

During the wait he cursed a lot: at the crowds, at the town, at Route 133, at the volunteer fire department. Most of all, he cursed at himself. He knew all the roads in Bridgewater, especially the backcountry ones, that would have circumvented the traffic. He could have made it to Trooper Walker's house in ten minutes. Not forty.

Traffic was slowest in front of the firehouse, where the fair's entrance was set up. Through his open windows he could hear tinny music from the amusement rides, frightened bellows from the show animals, intermittent car horns, and the hushed, barely contained roar of ten thousand voices. The air smelled of barbecue chicken, roasting peanuts, popcorn, and hot pie. The lights caught his eyes, entrancing them: glittering Ferris wheel, red striped tents, pink cotton candy. It was all so hokey and ridiculously tinsel that it looked like tremendous fun. He wondered if he'd be able to take Amanda there, Saturday night or Sunday afternoon, before he had to leave Bridgewater.

Leave it forever, he grimly noted.

He couldn't find a parking spot in front of Trooper Walker's house, so he kept going. He found an opening about three hundred yards farther on the left. To get it, he had to pull a quick U-turn and double back, cutting off two girls in a red pickup truck. They flashed the finger in unison, and held it up long after he had gotten out of his car and locked up. Traffic was moving just as slowly from this end, so he got another look at their middle fingers, nails chewed to the cuticle, flaking purple polish, as he walked past them. One of them shouted: "Nice Day-Glo shirt, faggot." He smiled and waved to show the comment didn't bother him. Secretly, he wished he had changed his shirt.

Trooper Walker's house was lit up like he owned a majority share of Connecticut Light and Power: front lights, lawn spots, and a walkway lantern all ablaze. The kids in the neighborhood could have played a night ball game in the yard. Before he stepped into the glow, he checked for Dorothy in the Village Store lot. He didn't see her, and figured she was probably delayed by the same traffic that had just ensnared him.

The door to the house was open, so he stepped up to the screen. A baseball game was on, the drone of the announcer's voice too low to distinguish the team. He rapped on the metal frame and yelled out: "Hello? Trooper Walker?"

The dogs charged the door, howling insanely, then a woman's voice shouted: "Coming."

A few seconds later, Trooper Walker's wife turned the corner, looking gussied up for the fair. She had squeezed into a tight red sequined blouse, denim miniskirt, and a pair of silver-tipped cowgirl boots. Her hair looked blonder, and kinkier from a recent perm. The smile on her face froze when she saw him. She didn't speak, so he said: "Evening, Ms. Walker. Is your husband home?"

"He's watching TV."

"Could I speak to him?"

"He's watchin' the ball game."

Unsure of whether that meant yes or no, Carpo put his hand on the door. He smiled and pushed it open, asking, "May I?"

She stepped aside, and he stepped in. The dogs went right for his crotch; he shoved them away. Trooper Walker's voice floated over the television sound. "Kat, who is it?"

"It's the man from the city," she shouted back. "The reporter. He wants to speak to you."

"Pain in the ass," Trooper Walker muttered loud enough for Carpo to hear. His wife nodded, as if to show solidarity with her husband's assessment. Before he appeared, Carpo heard him say to someone: "Wait here, I'll get rid of him."

Trooper Walker was out of uniform, and by the look of things, off for the night. He was wearing a plain white T-shirt and blue jeans, toting a can of Miller lite. By his breath and red eyes, Carpo figured it wasn't his first beer of the night.

"What do you want?"

"Sorry to bother you so late, but I hear Trent Donovan turned up this afternoon. I was wondering if I could speak to him."

Trooper Walker sipped from the can, foamy white specks appeared in the corners of his mouth. He wiped them off with the back of his hand, then wiped his hands on his T-shirt. "Where'd you hear that?"

"I heard it from a woman in New Milford."

The trooper's eyes narrowed, as if he couldn't decide whether to believe him or not. "What's it to you if he is here?"

"I need to ask him a few questions."

"Nope," Trooper Walker said, punctuating the rejection with a burp. "That journalism crap might work in the city, but it won't get you squat 'round here."

"So I've seen," Carpo muttered, needled. "Then maybe you could just pass along a message."

"Depends."

"Could you tell him that I was sorting through some of Jack's papers this afternoon and found a legal document. I think he's going to need it Monday."

"What's Monday?"

"The lease renewal for Southville comes due. He didn't tell you that?"

"You mean Southville, the drowned town?"

"Yeah, there's a lease on the property beneath the lake. On Monday it expires. I can't believe he—"

"Just a second there," a voice interrupted from the living room. "Trooper Walker, I'll speak to the young man."

The new Trent Donovan turned the corner in the hallway; as Carpo had guessed, he'd been listening the entire time. He looked mid to late sixties, six feet tall, and walked with the ease of a born athlete. He had thinning gray hair, soft brown eyes, and he kept his head tilted to the side, almost parallel to his shoulder, as if he were peering through a mailbox slot.

"How do you do, Mr. Donovan?" Carpo extended his hand. "My name is Michael Carpo."

The man's hand was as soft as a surgeon's. "Michael Carpo," he said, smiling. "Pleased to make your acquaintance."

"I'm a friend of Jack Crawford's, or at least I was. I used to watch his cottage every summer. I was the one who found the body Sunday."

"Terrible, just terrible," the man said grimly. "I can't believe it happened, and so close to the end of all this. Forty years of waiting, it just seems too cruel to me."

"Have you been in Bridgewater this whole time?"

"No, I abandoned ship two years ago. It was getting too crazy here. Been bouncing around ever since, all over the county, too scared to put down for more than a couple of months." The man took a step closer. "Now, tell me about this document. You found it in Jack's possession?"

"Jack's family asked me to sift through his personal papers before they sell the cottage. I found a document in the desk. It looks like a lease rider, and it's supposed to go with the current Lillinonah renewal."

"And what's it about?"

"It's in some pretty dense legalese, but from what I could make out, it specifies the manner in which the papers are supposed to be filed on Monday. I guess Jack hired a lawyer to reword some of the language in the original."

The man's brown pupils hardened into small black points. "Jack was always pulling funny business like this. Anyway, what's done is done. Can I have a look at it please?"

"Oh, I don't have it on me, Mr. Donovan. I was too scared to carry it on my person. Don't worry, though, it's in a safe place."

"Where?"

"I locked it inside Jack's desk."

The man smiled. "I'd sure like a chance to see it before Monday."

"I could drop it off in the morning."

"No, you don't have to go through that much trouble. I'll drive by myself. Is nine-thirty too early?"

Carpo shook his head no.

"And you're sure it's safe in that desk, right? I wouldn't want anything to happen to it before Monday." The man looked at Trooper Walker. "We've had enough surprises this week as it is."

"Don't worry," Carpo said, "it's safe."

They shook hands, then walked to the screen door. "Thanks for coming over," the man said, "and while you're here, you should drop in on the fair. The VFD puts on a real fine show."

"I plan to." Carpo glanced at his watch. "In fact, my date's waiting as we speak. Trooper Walker, Mr. Donovan, have a good night."

Carpo backed out the door and down the front steps. The traffic had died down a bit, but there were still hundreds of cars parked along the curb. At first he didn't spot Dorothy anywhere among them, but at the bottom of the steps a flashing headlight caught his eye, flicking on and off in the Village Store parking lot. He waved at the lights, which belonged to a classic 1950s black Buick with shiny chrome bumpers and a polished chrome grille. A second later Dorothy's head leaned out the window, and she waved back.

"Who's that?" Trooper Walker asked.

Carpo turned back to the house, until that moment unaware that the trooper had been watching. "Um, she's my date."

"She looks kind of old," he said, his mouth forming a smirk. "Maybe she's too old and blind to notice that hot pink shirt of yours."

Carpo ignored the comment. He jogged across the street and climbed into the passenger seat of the Buick. The massive door swung shut with the solid clank of a bank vault.

"That's some wild shirt you're wearing, dear," Dorothy said.

"I wasn't planning on wearing it out," he said, annoyed. "So where've you been?"

"Where have I been? Where have *I* been? How about waiting at the library all day for you to call. How about at my house, lying to my husband about where I was going at nine o'clock at night." Dorothy stared out the windshield, wide-eyed, hands gripping the wheel as if she needed to steady herself. "Do you know he actually accused me of having an affair."

"Who did?"

"My husband. We've been married fifty-two years, and tonight he asks if I'm running around on him. Can you imagine that?"

"Who would you be running around with?"

"You. He thinks I'm having an affair with you."

Carpo studied Dorothy's face for a signal of distress or anger. All he saw, though, was the red flush of excitement.

She began to snicker through her nose, quiet piggish snorts that made him giggle too. Suddenly, everything seemed hilarious, and they both succumbed to a boisterous laugh. After a day of such intense pressures, the release felt wonderful to Carpo.

"Imagine when he meets you," she said hoarsely, tears streaming down her cheeks, "and sees how young you are. He'll think I'm some kind of a letch. It's like *Tea and Sympathy*, only you're fifty years my junior."

"Seriously, Dorothy, I hope he's not too angry at me."

"He'll get over it," she said, waving her hand. "Besides, I'm enjoying myself. I haven't had this much fun since I was a teeny-bopper."

"Frankly, I wouldn't mind if things quieted down a bit." His face grew serious. "Did you bring that photo of the group?"

"It's right here."

She retrieved an envelope from the glove compartment and handed it to him. Inside, he found the *New Milford Times* photograph of the victorious members of Justice for Southville. He held it at an angle to capture some of the light filtering in from the streetlamp. The shadows made the faces of the people look like a row of dark smudges.

"Do you have an interior light?" he asked.

Dorothy tapped a button on the left side of the steering wheel; a bright overhead came on, transforming the dark smudges into faces. Jack's proud smile beamed from the middle of the row, his black stogie poised defiantly between his teeth. Elizabeth Jessup stood to his right, wearing a gray suit and a pillbox hat. He recognized Fern Gimlins too. He was two down from Elizabeth Jessup, face rigid and unsmiling, as if the idea of having his picture taken literally terrified him. Carpo read the names in the photo caption at the bottom for Trent Donovan's, and then he counted across the row of faces until he found him, fifth from the right. He stared hard at the man, something about it bothering him.

"Well?" Dorothy asked impatiently. "Which one is Trent Donovan?"

"Hang on."

The face was too smudged to determine the correct man, but there was no hiding his height. The Trent Donovan in the photograph was roughly the same height as Jack Crawford. Jack had been a few inches shorter than Carpo, meaning that the Trent Donovan he had met first, the one confined to a walker, was the real Trent Donovan.

So who was the man at Trooper Walker's house? Was he a complete impostor? Someone who had never been associated with Justice for Southville but perhaps hoped to cash in on the lease renewal money?

He went back over the photo, studying the height of each person. The third man on the left, two over from Jack, was the tallest. He also had a head that was tilted to the side, almost shyly, on his shoulders.

He pushed the photograph in front of Dorothy and tapped his finger on the face of Claudell Jenkins. "That's him," he said. "The man in Trooper Walker's house is Claudell Jenkins. The one who supposedly killed himself two years ago by jumping off the Lake Lillinonah bridge."

Dorothy squinted at the photo for a long while. "Are you sure?"

He nodded.

"What does it mean?"

"I don't know yet. Maybe he planned a fake suicide so he could hide out and protect himself."

"Then why would he come back as Trent Donovan and not himself?"

They looked at each other, both thinking the same thing. After a full minute of silence Dorothy asked: "So what should we do?"

"I don't think there's any use dragging this out. I'll just take this photo inside and confront him. If he can come up with a suitable explanation, then we'll know why he's pretending to be someone else."

"And if he can't, you won't have to look far for a trooper."

Carpo frowned. "Unless they're in it together, in cahoots, I mean. Fern Gimlins told me more than one person attacked him. And Trooper Walker was the one who found Claudell Jenkins's clothes, shoes, and suicide note on Lake Lillinonah bridge. Not to mention that he requested this photo from the library two years ago."

"I don't like you going in there, Carpo, not a bit. Why don't we call the police and have them come over and straighten this out. Just in case."

He had to agree with her; it was the safest way to handle the situation. He opened the car door, folding the photograph in half and sticking it in his shirt pocket. "What time is it?" he asked.

"Ten to nine."

He thought of Amanda, sitting at the cottage alone, waiting for him to return. He had to warn her that their dinner plans would have to apply to another night. "Can I borrow a quarter?"

"Just dial 911."

"I'll call the cops in a minute, but first I've got to make a personal call."

She reached under the overstuffed seat and pulled out a large shoulder purse. She opened it and felt blindly among the items. The scent of peppermint filled the air as she sifted through handfuls of throat lozenges, bobby pins, tissue packs, and loose change. She extracted a quarter from the detritus and handed it to him. He walked across the lot to the telephone booth, dropped the coin in the slot, and dialed the cottage.

On the twentieth ring Amanda answered. Her voice sounded strange as she exclaimed: "Carpo, thank God it's you!"

"What's the matter?"

"It's Trent Donovan. He called here a second ago. He says there's an emergency."

His hand tightened on the phone. "What's wrong?"

"He says a car just pulled into the driveway with the lights turned off. We've got to help him. He's really, really scared."

"Did you call the police?"

"I couldn't get his address, he was too panicked. Give me it now, so I can call them."

"It's 1170 Obtuse Rocks Road. It's in Brookfield, so call the barracks there. Tell them to send a squad car right away."

"What are you going to do?"

"I'm going there right now."

Eighteen

Dorothy pushed the Buick hard on the drive to Brookfield, her body perched at the edge of the seat cushion, eyes barely clearing the steering wheel. The car's eight cylinder engine screamed like a jet turbine, the chassis and seat springs creaking every time they skidded around a corner. Within ten minutes they had crossed the Lillinonah bridge and turned left onto Obtuse Rocks Road.

"It's a quarter-mile down on the right," he said. "Number 1170."

She found the driveway marker and started up for the house, gravel clunking like hammer blows on the bottom of the car. Halfway up, he tapped her arm and pointed at the old logging trail.

"Turn off the headlights and pull in there," he commanded. "I want to take this quietly, just in case we've arrived before the cops."

She killed the lights and steered off the driveway into the woods. She coasted for a bit with the clutch depressed, the reflection off the chrome bumper helping to illuminate the trail, then she circled behind a dogwood tree. Before he could slip out of the car, she grabbed his arm. "Be careful up there."

He nodded, too nervous to speak. He held in the door handle as he closed the door, then slipped through the trees, making his way to the cabin. A full moon had risen, bright enough to see his way through the woods; it also made the palm trees on his shirt glow like neon lighting. As he jogged along, he removed his shirt and flipped it inside out. The bright colors still showed, but not the fluorescence.

The cabin loomed before him, a square black shadow at the top of the clearing. There was only one car in the driveway, Mr. Donovan's light blue Toyota; he wondered if he had arrived too late. He bypassed the front door and circled to the backyard, pressing against the cabin to conceal his body in the shadows. He kept his ears tuned for sound, any sound, inside or outside the cabin. Nothing competed with the pulse pounding in his ears. When he reached the bay window, he averted his eyes from the living room; he dreaded the thought of finding another body, the fourth in a week. Finally, he held his breath and forced himself to look through the windows.

Trent Donovan was there, lying almost supine in his reclining chair. His eyes were closed, his head tilted on his shoulder. Carpo watched him closely, looking for signs of death. Though motionless and pale, there were no visible signs of blood or bruising. Was he still alive? Carpo scrambled for a closer look, peering now through the door. The man's chest appeared to bob and a small object on his stomach moved up and down. Relief flowed through him like a stiff drink. *It's a book,* he realized. *Trent fell asleep while reading.*

Carpo tapped on the glass, causing the old man to lurch up in his chair. He looked like a grizzly emerging from hibernation; hair frazzled, eyes puffy, jaw deformed with yawning. He stared around the living room, befuddled, until his eyes came to rest on the door. Carpo waved, but Trent did not acknowledge the gesture. He snared his walker, hoisted himself out of the chair, and then hobbled to the door.

It took several seconds before Carpo realized that Trent couldn't see him. The light from inside the living room turned the windows into one-way mirrors, allowing him to see inside the cabin but Trent to see only his own reflection. Instead of knocking, Carpo shouted, "It's me, Mr. Donovan, Michael Carpo."

Recognizing the voice, Trent's face collapsed into a scowl. He pressed his nose to the glass and studied Carpo, then unlocked the door. "What the hell are you doing out there?" he asked. "You scared the crap out of me."

Carpo stepped into the living room, looking all around. "Is everything okay? Are you safe?"

Something flashed in Trent's hands, then something cold pressed into Carpo's stomach. It was a pistol, a Smith and Wesson .38 Special, its ugly snub nose stuck deep in his gut.

Carpo raised his arms reflexively. "Whoa, whoa, hang on. It's only me. Michael Carpo."

"I know you," Trent said matter-of-factly, "but not enough to trust you. I didn't stay alive two whole years now by trusting people. Now, what are you doing sneaking around my backyard?"

Try as he might, Carpo could not raise his eyes from the gun. Nor could he lower his arms. "I can explain, Mr. Donovan, I can explain everything. But please stop pointing that at me."

Trent stepped back, lowered the gun. "All right, over

there," he said, using the pistol like a finger to point at the couch. "We'll sit and have a chat."

As Carpo walked to the couch, arms still in the air, he said: "Glad to see guns really terrify you."

"They do. That's why I have one myself."

Carpo sat on the couch. Everything looked the same in the cabin. Obviously Trent was no longer in serious trouble. He waited until Trent had lowered himself into the reclining chair, then asked, "So what happened to the car?"

"What car?"

"The one that pulled in the driveway with the lights off."

"What on earth are you talking about?"

Carpo blinked several times, trying to make sense of the answer. "Didn't you call the cottage a little while ago saying that a car had pulled in the driveway with the lights off?"

"Hell no. I've been sitting here the entire evening reading a biography on Bowie Kuhn. His story puts me out every time. I didn't wake up until you started busting through the door."

"I wasn't busting through. I was knocking."

"Sounded a lot worse to me."

"Either way, you'd better put that gun away. I had someone call 911. The police should be here in a couple of minutes."

Trent glared at him, gun still aimed in his vicinity. "You know something, I'm starting to have my doubts about you."

Carpo chuckled nervously. "You don't really think I'm involved with this, do you?"

"I don't know. This afternoon I didn't, but after you left, I got to thinking. You were the one who found Jack's body on Sunday, you were the last person to see Bethie alive on Monday, and you found Fern on Thursday. Three bodies in five days, that's not a positive statistic. And now I catch you sneaking around my own backyard." Trent shook his head. "Yes, I'm having doubts."

"If I were planning on murdering you, why didn't I do it this afternoon? We were here all alone. Why would I wait until now?"

Trent shrugged. "I didn't say I had all the answers. Just questions. A lot of them."

Carpo remembered the photograph tucked in his shirt pocket. He took it out, unfolded it, and handed it to Trent. "I'm sure you've seen this before, it was on the front page of *The New Milford Times* after your group won its suit against the state." He paused a few seconds so Trent could get a look at the photograph. "Tonight a man who fits the height and general appearance of Claudell Jenkins showed up at Trooper Walker's house. He's asking for protection until Monday."

"It can't be Claudell, he's dead."

"Oh, he's not going by the name Claudell Jenkins. He's using your name . . . Trent Donovan."

Trent didn't show any visible emotion, but Carpo knew his mind was in overdrive, because he set the gun in his lap and reached for the pipe on the table. Without lifting his eyes, he asked, "You sure it's Claudell?"

"Far as I can tell. The photo's old, but it sure looks like him."

Trent mumbled something unintelligible.

"Pardon, Mr. Donovan?"

"I said, I knew it."

"Knew what?"

Trent clamped the pipe between his teeth. "Me and Jack,

we always speculated it might be someone from the group. It's the only way they could have gotten past all our locks and dogs and guns. Everybody was so scared about dying, they never trusted strangers. It had to be someone they all knew." Trent shook his head forlornly. "All this time, and the poison was in us."

"That's why I'm here. A little while ago someone called the cottage claiming to be you, and claiming to be in trouble. I told the person . . ."

Carpo's voice trailed off; Trent wasn't listening. "Mr. Donovan, are you okay?"

The pipe fell from Trent's mouth to his lap, where the gun still lay. His eyes looked unfocused and he murmured gibberish. Carpo walked to him. "It's going to be okay now, you're finally safe. When the police arrive, we'll show them that picture and take them over to Trooper Walker's house to confront Claudell Jenkins in person."

He patted the man's shoulder; the contact seemed to push him into an abyss. A tremble went through his body, like wobbly Jell-O, and the gun and pipe clattered to the floor.

"Mr. Donovan? You okay?"

Tires slashed through the gravel, and a pair of headlights swept across the windows.

"Can you hear me, Mr. Donovan? The police are here. Everything's going to be fine. I'll be right back."

He walked to the front door, the old feeling of inadequacy seeping into him. Once again the words weren't there for him. He wanted to assure the man that he was not alone, that he would stick by him and make sure that everything worked out, but he didn't know *how* to say it.

A state trooper was waiting on the stoop when he opened the door, a middle-aged white man about the same height as Carpo, his hat gripped politely in his hands. "Evening," the trooper said. "Is Trent Donovan here?"

"Yes, he's inside. What took you so long to get here? We called almost an hour ago."

He peered past the officer, looking for his partner. There wasn't a partner, nor was there a squad car. Just a dark green sedan. Puzzled, he asked: "Are you from the Brookfield barracks?"

The man answered by raising the felt hat. His right hand clenched a hunting knife with a ten-inch jagged blade. Carpo recoiled at the sight. His eyes ran from the knife up the man's body to the silver nameplate pinned to his chest. What he saw there made his own chest burn so badly that he almost wondered if he'd been stabbed: Trooper Chester Cutler.

He realized he recognized the name: Trooper Chester Cutler. It was Amanda's father.

Nineteen

Once the initial shock of seeing Amanda's father had passed, an odd sensation of tranquillity came over Carpo. All his fear and anxiety evaporated. He felt supremely calm. Almost peaceful.

No doubt, this reaction was due to his mind playing tricks with his body, signaling some gland to dump massive amounts of adrenaline into his bloodstream, preventing him from running, screaming, or even begging for mercy. Or, perhaps, the reason for his composure was purely due to resolution: He no longer wondered what Jack's killer looked like. Over the past five days, his imagination had pumped up the killer to superhuman levels in both physical and intellectual capabilities. Contrasting that image now was the man who stood before him, gripping a knife in one hand and a wilted state trooper's hat in the other. Face-to-face with Chester Cutler, Carpo found his adversary somewhat of a disappointment.

He was short and very thin, with clumps of brown hair that fell unevenly down his forehead. His pale skin was stretched tautly over his cheekbones, pulling his nose so crooked that his left nostril lay flat against the right one. His mouth twitched and his small gray eyes flitted about the cabin. He seemed so disheveled and nervous that under other circumstances, Carpo might have felt sorry for the man.

"Where's Trent Donovan?" Trooper Cutler repeated, holding the knife in full view. It was an old hunting knife, the top of its silver blade notched for a thumb grip. The cutting edge itself looked well worn, scratched along the sides, probably from the countless times it had been dragged across a sharpening stone.

"He's inside," Carpo said, feeling as if his voice had emanated from a million miles away.

"Let's go."

Trooper Cutler tilted the knife up in his fist and shoved Carpo with his knuckles. Carpo stumbled into the living room and took a seat on the couch. Trooper Cutler circled the reclining chair and the couch, looking between Carpo and Trent, as if he were the one awaiting instructions. Finally, Trooper Cutler pointed at Trent Donovan and asked, "What's up with him?"

Carpo looked at Trent, surprised to see that something was seriously wrong with him. His body had collapsed against the chair's padded arm, head tilted onto one shoulder, and his eyes rolled up into his forehead. He seemed to be laboring to catch his breath, mouth open, making tiny moaning noises as if his belly ached. Carpo moved as if to assist him, but Trooper Cutler shouted, "Sit down!" Carpo sank back to the couch.

Trooper Cutler kneeled before the chair, bringing his face level to Trent's. He shifted his head from side to side, peering into each of Trent's vacant eyes. Something about the old man amused the trooper, and his bony cheeks disappeared in a bulge of flesh, mouth grinning wider and wider.

"What's the matter, Trent? You gone sick on me? Come on, old boy, look who's here to see you. Remember me? Think back, way back, to the little boy who used to shoot Karla Phelan's cats with a BB gun."

The trooper's face was an inch from Trent's, but it didn't seem as if he could hear anything. His breath came in ragged gasps and his forehead glistened with sweat. Carpo started to wonder if Trent had suffered a heart attack.

"And how about the night Karla Phelan died? Remember her, Trenty? The bitty who got her throat slit? Now you starting to remember who I am?"

Trooper Cutler lifted the knife to Trent's face, angling the blade so it would glint in the man's eyes. "I brought you a little present, Trent. Lookie here at this. Ain't it pretty? I got it at Fern's store fifty years ago. Remember that, Trent, 'cause you were there. Fact, you and Fern made fun of me. Said I'd just end up cutting myself with it. Well, guess what, old boy? Today it's you that's going to get the cutting."

The trooper's voice had grown deeper, as if he were summoning the hatred from deep within himself. Carpo wondered if he had killed the others this way, standing over them, reciting past insults suffered at the hands of the other residents of Southville. Carpo recalled that Amanda had said her family was from the area. It never occurred to him that they might have come from Southville.

Suddenly, Carpo remembered the pistol. Trent had dropped it just before Carpo had gone to answer the door. He leaned forward and checked around the couch, but didn't see it. He wondered if it had gotten kicked under the couch.

"And you know what's going to happen after that, Trenty? Me and your old pal, Claudell Jenkins, we're going to collect that lease money and split it. How does that make you feel? Knowing that one of your own helped kill all the members of your group?"

Carpo leaned far off the couch, searching the floor for the pistol. Out of the corner of his eye, he saw Trooper Cutler grab Trent around the neck, the knife clenched in his fist as if he intended to punch the blade through Trent's face. The trooper seemed oblivious of Carpo's presence, so Carpo dropped to his knees and started feeling beneath the couch for the gun.

"What in the hell are you doing?" Trooper Cutler shouted, catching Carpo with both arms beneath the couch. He grabbed Carpo by a clump of hair and yanked him to his feet, then shoved him on the couch. "What were you looking for down there? Huh? Answer me, you glow in the dark moron."

"Excuse me, officer," Trent Donovan announced in a flat, chilling voice. "This is what he's looking for."

Both Trooper Cutler and Carpo turned to find Trent with the pistol cupped in his hands. Cutler's eyes flapped wide, his back stiffening like a steel rod.

There was a period of two or three seconds where all three of them held absolutely still, their minds racing to comprehend the sudden shift in fortunes. Carpo was feeling delirious now that he realized he was going to keep living. Trooper Cutler, on the other hand, must have been grappling with the realization that he would be spending the rest of his life rotting in a prison cell. At least, that's what he and Carpo figured during those few everlasting seconds.

"This is from Jack Crawford," Trent whispered a second before his finger curled against the trigger.

The explosion from the end of the gun was deafening. Trooper Cutler whirled in a complete circle, then fell as if he'd been decked by a heavyweight roundhouse. His face registered shock when he looked at his left arm. The bullet had pulverized his biceps, leaving his arm dangling.

"And Bethie Jessup sends her regards with—"

Trent's last words were engulfed by the next explosion. It didn't sound as loud as the first, mostly because Carpo's ears were ringing, but the impact was just as devastating. The bullet struck the trooper's right thigh, splattering blood across the front of his uniform and pants. He squealed loud and high, like a butchered hog; Carpo wondered if it was from the pain or the realization that he would never get a chance to rot inside that prison cell.

"Charlotte Thigpen and Karla Phelan autographed this one."

A yellow flame spat from the barrel, and the bullet struck somewhere in the trooper's abdomen. His body folded and arms flew into the air as if he had been kicked in the gut.

"And I best not forget my old friend Fern. Yes, he sold you that knife, Trooper Cutler, but guess what else he did?"

The pistol rose in a slow, calculated motion. Trent's left eye squinted shut as he drew a bead on the narrow target before him.

"Old Fern gave me this gun," he said. He paused for a second, gun pointed right at the trooper's forehead. Carpo prayed that he would stop, but the man's upper lips curled high above his teeth as he snarled, "You son of a bitch."

Trooper Cutler's skull exploded like a dynamited watermelon. Carpo saw the impact, the rupture of bone and spray of fluid, before he squeezed his eyes shut so tightly that little white dots flashed inside his eyelids. He heard Trent Donovan wheeze painfully, then a clatter as the gun hit the floor. It landed near Carpo's leg, acrid smoke curling up from the barrel.

Carpo stayed like that for what felt like hours, eyes sealed tight, hands clamped over his face, until he heard the far-off wail of a siren.

Twenty

Dorothy led the charge of state troopers into the cabin. She looked like Medusa's grandmother, teeth bared, writhing gray hair, eyes fiercely searching among the carnage for Carpo. When she spotted him, she rushed over and threw her arms around him. She insisted he was injured, trusting in his well-being only after several minutes spent embracing him. Carpo could only imagine what her husband would have said if he had been present.

The Brookfield troopers kept their nine-millimeters drawn, square barrels pointed at the floor, until Trent's .38 was recovered. Then one of them went to the front door and waved a battery of paramedics into the room. The paramedics rushed straight to Trent's aid, opening his shirt, checking his pulse and blood pressure. It turned out that his heart was fine, he was suffering from severe shock. Carpo wondered if they would have arrived at the same diagnosis if they had seen him massacre Trooper Cutler ten minutes earlier.

The windows facing the driveway flashed with dozens of spinning lights as more emergency vehicles arrived and more uniformed people flooded the cabin. Each person seemed to have a pre-assigned task, which they set about accomplishing in silence. They photographed the room and the position of Trooper Cutler, they searched the cabin, they fingerprinted the doorknobs and inspected the windows, they questioned Carpo, Trent, and Dorothy, and then they bagged the body.

Carpo was thankful to have Dorothy next to him through it all. The calm he had experienced just a short time ago had been a mere facade. Realizing his close brush with death, his muscles turned spastic. Suddenly, he couldn't stop shaking. Dorothy held his hand while the troopers questioned him; he felt silly, but it did keep his hands steady. It was during the questioning that he learned how she had summoned the troopers to the cabin.

She had been parked in the turnoff, waiting for the police to arrive, when Trooper Cutler drove past with his headlights turned off. Sensing that something was amiss, she had gone in search of help, stumbling across two officers writing a speeding ticket near Brookfield center. She must have sounded pretty convincing, because the officers had stopped what they were doing and followed her directly to the cabin.

The most surprising arrival that night—after Trooper Cutler, of course—was Trooper Walker. He rushed into the cabin ten minutes after the last trooper, eyes bloodshot, uniform untucked. When he walked past, Carpo got a whiff of beer on his breath; he looked tipsy enough to flunk a Breathalyzer. When he saw Carpo on the couch, sitting next to the puddle of Chester Cutler's brains, he sobered instantly.

"What the hell are you doing here?"

Carpo, exhausted and in no mood for trouble from the

trooper, said, "It's a long story, but I guess you'd better listen to it, since you're a big part of it."

Trooper Walker started to say something; Carpo held up his hand to shut him up. Then he pointed at Trent Donovan, sitting in a reclining chair, calmly puffing his pipe. "You should introduce yourself to him, Trooper Walker. Heck, you really should recognize him. His name is Trent Donovan. The *real* Trent Donovan."

"Then who's the fellow at my place?"

"His name is Claudell Jenkins. He's one of the original members of Justice for Southville. But you know that already, you're the one who found his clothes on the Lake Lillinonah bridge. He faked his own suicide two winters ago by making it look like he jumped into the lake."

Trooper Walker blinked a few times, incredulous. "Then who the hell is that?" he asked, pointing at the body bag.

"It's State Trooper Chester Cutler. You probably know him, since he grew up in Southville and lived in Bridgewater a few years. He and Claudell Jenkins were murdering the members of Justice for Southville so they could take all the money from the renewal of the Lake Lillinonah lease."

"Well, I'll be." Trooper Walker pulled his hat off, scratched at the indentation left by the brim. "Why would Claudell go through all that trouble to kill himself on the Lillinonah bridge?"

"That's a good question. He must have thought he could maneuver more easily if people thought he was dead. But you can ask him that in person when you get back to your house."

"I'll do that, the lying bastard."

"You'd better be careful, Trooper Walker, he's probably handy with a knife."

"Don't you worry none, Carpo, I'll take care of him."

Trooper Walker tensed his jaw, setting his face as hard as cement. The way he looked, Carpo imagined he would, indeed, take care of Claudell Jenkins.

All in all, the Brookfield troopers didn't make Carpo stay very long. After asking a few more questions they took down his name, social security number, address, and telephone number in New York City, then they said he could leave. Before he did, he made sure Trent had fully recovered.

The old man seemed a bit quiet but, all things considered, in fine condition. He stayed in the reclining chair, pipe oozing aromatic smoke, as he watched the activity in the cabin. His eyes were relaxed, almost indifferent to the activity, a stark contrast to the sickly expression he had exhibited while Trooper Cutler was waving a knife at his throat. Carpo wondered if the expression and the hyperventilating had all been trickery, an attempt to throw Cutler off his guard long enough to use the pistol.

About an hour after witnessing Chester Cutler's skull disintegrate, Carpo said good-bye to Trent Donovan, Trooper Walker, and the other troopers, and left the cabin. Too tired to drive all the way to his car in Bridgewater Center, he asked Dorothy to drop him at the cottage. She offered to take him to his car the next morning.

The night's events had done little to subdue Dorothy. On the drive home she chattered on about all sorts of things, either not noticing or not caring about his silence. He didn't pay attention. He kept his eyes out the window, watching the tree shadows and aluminum guardrails flicker past, as he decided on the best way to deal with Amanda.

It didn't take prescience or even an overabundance of intuition to realize that she had set him up. Knowing that he would call to check in at some point, she had told him that Trent Donovan was in trouble and needed the address so she could call the police. Then, he guessed, she had passed the address along to her father so he could finish his plot against the last member of Justice for Southville. Carpo hadn't told anyone about his suspicion, not the Brookfield troopers, Trooper Walker, Trent Donovan, not even Dorothy. It was a problem that he needed to solve on his own.

When they pulled up to the cottage, the interior lights were turned off and Amanda's car was gone. He wasn't surprised; she would have been a fool to stick around the place, especially since she probably believed him to be dead. Dorothy didn't want to drop him at an empty house, but he convinced her that he would be fine. He thanked her for the ride and promised to call in the morning so they could pick up the car. She kept the headlights pointed at the front door until he unlocked it.

As soon as he stepped inside the cottage, he sensed that something was wrong. He'd been gone most of the day, yet Floyd wasn't there to greet him. Normally, the dog would have been standing at the door, waiting to pounce on him. He waited just inside the kitchen, ears tuned for any noises as he considered whether to walk farther into the cottage. He looked up the driveway, where the Buick's red taillights faded around the corner; now he had no choice but to enter the house.

A strange noise, a faint clicking sound, came from the

living room. He flicked the light switch on, but the kitchen remained in darkness. He placed his keys on the butcher block and strained to read the clock over the stove: 8:55 P.M. The cottage had been without power almost since he had called Amanda from the Village Store parking lot.

The clicking noise started again, and he knew it was Floyd scratching at something in the living room. He wanted to call to the dog but he remained silent, fearful of what might lie between them. He felt along the butcher block until he found the knife drawer, then picked through the knives by touch. He chose the largest knife, a J. A. Henckel butcher knife with a fourteen-inch razor-sharp blade. He held the knife away from his body and started for the living room.

The moon was still over the valley, its faint light reflecting off the lake and filtering through the large bay windows. He stood at the entrance to the living room, trying to spot where Floyd was, when the clicking noise started again. He almost dropped the knife when he realized where it was coming from: *Floyd is in the bathroom.*

He edged along the wall until he reached the door to the bathroom. "What's the matter, boy?" he whispered. "You okay, Floyd?" The dog whined, then the clicking noises resumed; Floyd was scratching the tile floor.

He entered the bathroom, both hands extended in front of him, trying to feel if anything was in his path. The moon didn't reach this side of the cottage, so the bathroom was much darker than the living room. So dark, in fact, that he couldn't see his outstretched hands. After three shuffled steps, his knee bumped into Floyd. He knelt beside the dog and patted his head. The dog whined, then lunged toward the linen closet and resumed scratching the floor; it was as if the dog were trying to tunnel beneath the door. Carpo pulled him back by the collar and hugged him, trying to calm him, as he listened for any sound. A tree branch scraped on the roof and the cottage itself settled with an audible creak, but inside the closet, where Floyd wanted so badly to get, it was silent.

As soon as he opened the door, Floyd leapt inside. He followed on his hands and knees, crawling on the cold, hard tile, until his right hand collided with an object. He grabbed it, realizing that it was a human foot. A sneaker covered the foot, by the feel of the waffled sole a running shoe. A second later Carpo smelled familiar perfume. *It's Amanda.*

He grabbed her by the ankle and dragged her out of the closet into the living room. In the weak light he could see that her eyes were closed, her face very pale. He groped along the side of her neck, feeling for the carotid artery. It pulsed against his fingers with a reassuring strength. As he put a pillow beneath her head, he noticed the blood caked in her hair. He ran to the telephone and dialed 911, not realizing until the phone was against his ear that the line was dead.

He went back to Amanda, brushed the hair off her face, massaged her temples. Floyd licked her cheeks, whining softly, urging her to awaken. Her eyes quivered, the pupils moving beneath the lids as if she were having a bad dream, but they didn't open.

"Come on, Amanda," he whispered, "wake up. We've got to get out of here. Please, wake up."

The nearest neighbor was a quarter-mile away. He had no chance of carrying her there, but he didn't want to leave her either, not in her current condition. No car, no telephone, no electricity, he scrambled his brain trying to think of a way to summon help.

Floyd stopped licking Amanda's face and walked toward the kitchen. A few seconds passed before Carpo noticed that the dog's ears were back, his head cocked a little to the side, as if trying to distinguish a very faint noise. A moment later Carpo heard it. A pair of footsteps coming across the driveway, then across the flagstones leading to the kitchen. Someone was about to enter the cottage.

He patted his hands wildly around Amanda's body, panicked as he realized that the knife was still in the bathroom. He scrambled across the floor, into the bathroom, and fumbled around the linen closet until he found the knife, then he carried it back to the living room and kneeled beside Amanda. Part of him felt like tossing away the knife, as if its possession would guarantee violence; another part of him made him squeeze its handle so hard, his knuckles hurt, terrified by the thought of being caught defenseless.

Hinges creaked as the kitchen door swung open, and again as it swung closed. A flashlight beam swept over the kitchen, then it melded with the volume of the footsteps, growing louder and brighter as the person approached the living room. Carpo stayed where he was, mind and body frozen.

When the person reached the living room, the light was on Carpo's face. He couldn't see who was controlling it, all identity cloaked behind the powerful beam. The light played over him, studying his features. Finally, after what felt like hours, Claudell Jenkins said, "How about if you bring me that lease rider, son? I went all through that desk before you got here and couldn't find it."

Carpo brought his hand up to shield his eyes. "That's because it doesn't exist."

"Bullshit. There's no way you'd've gone all the way to Trooper Walker's house if there wasn't one. Now, where is it?"

"I'm telling you the truth. I made it up. I wanted to say something that would make you worried, make you do something brash. You can tear this place down to the foundation, you're not going to find it."

"I've got a better idea. Fetch the lease rider or I'll start slicing off your girlfriend's fingers, one every thirty seconds."

Carpo showed his own knife. "You'll have to get through me first."

The flashlight lowered and Claudell approached, his hulking physique moving with surprising agility. There was no doubt in Carpo's mind that Claudell was strong enough to wrestle the knife from him. He jumped to his feet when Claudell was five feet off and waved the knife side to side, as if he would slash him. Claudell chuckled. "Where'd you learn to handle a knife? Cub scouts? Put that thing down and go fetch me the rider. It'll save me some sweat, and you a lot of blood."

Carpo kept the knife where it was, stabbing at the air between them. Claudell inched forward, testing his will. He could see the man's face now; it was no longer smiling.

"Give me the knife. Hear me, son? Give me that damn knife."

Claudell put his hand out, palm up, and took another

step. Without thinking, Carpo plunged the knife into the outstretched hand, sinking the blade deep into the meat of his palm. Claudell screamed in agony; Carpo screamed in horror. It was an awful sensation, the knife plunging into living flesh. When Claudell tried to jerk his hand free, the action passed up the blade like an electric current. Carpo dropped the knife. It stayed in place, quivering in the palm. Claudell tugged it out and went for Carpo, both of them still screaming.

But a second before Claudell could reach him, Floyd sprung through the air and pounced on him. The dog looked like a werewolf—fangs bared, a strange roar emanating from his lungs. He leapt on Claudell's shoulders and flattened him to the ground. Carpo reached for the only decent weapon at hand: the heavy oak *forcola* on the mantel. He swung it like a war club, bashing Claudell's head over and over. Something inside him tried to hold back, a little voice that screamed: *Stop before you kill him!* But there was a much louder voice, a primal one, that howled in his ears, telling him to smash Claudell's skull and make sure the nightmare died forever.

It was Floyd that stopped him from killing Claudell. On one of his wild swings he accidentally plunked the dog on the snout. It must have smarted good, because Floyd yelped several times, snapping Carpo back to his senses.

He dropped the oarlock and sank to his knees, his body repulsed by what he'd almost done. His breath came in spasms. Claudell stayed motionless, his skull dripping blood.

Carpo had just enough presence of mind to run to the toilet before getting sick.

Twenty-one

On Sunday morning Carpo awoke with his limbs entwined with Amanda's as if they were an enormous ball of string: her leg flung over his hip, his knee hooked between her thighs, their arms locked behind each other's neck. She smelled fresh, and the way her skin melted into his triggered a wonderful sensation in him. A sensation of intimacy and warmth, of two bodies generating heat without effort. Even before his eyes opened, he thought: *What a wonderful way to wake up on my last morning in Bridgewater.*

They cuddled like that for an hour, pretending to be asleep as their limbs weaved and repositioned but never separated. He got her to open her eyes by running a line of kisses along the side of her neck. When he reached the lobe of her ear and began nibbling, her entire body shivered.

"Mmmm," she sighed. "What's your name, sailor?"

"Call me Ishmael," he said, then he opened his mouth and swallowed her earlobe.

"Carpo! Stop!" She covered her ears. "Gross, a wet willy on a Sunday morning."

"No better time for one."

He tried to pry her hands off her ears, but she flipped to her side, putting them face-to-face. She kissed him on the forehead, on each eye, and then on the mouth. He put his hands on her waist, pulling her close, then slowly ran them up her torso.

What a spectacular *way to awaken on my last day in Bridgewater.*

A day and a half had passed since he had come within inches of beating Claudell Jenkins to death. Though their fight had been a death match, he had suffered nothing more serious than a sore neck and a few scratches and bruises. In fact, his worst wound was an invisible one: He still cringed every time he remembered the sound the *forcola* had made cracking a home run against the man's skull.

She pulled back and smiled mischievously. "I think we should have coffee on the porch."

"Must we?"

"I don't want to spend the whole day in bed."

"Why not?"

She nudged him. "C'mon, make us some coffee. If you're a good boy, we can drink it here in bed."

He untangled himself from the sheets, slipped into a robe and slippers, and headed to the kitchen. Floyd raced ahead of him, his tail slapping happily against the walls. Carpo dumped two cups of kibble in the feed bowl, which Floyd pounced upon, jaws crunching noisily on the hard nuggets.

Carpo brewed ten cups of coffee, setting the entire carafe on a tray with two cups, spoons, milk, sugar, and a quartered brownie from the Village Store. As he carried the tray to the bedroom, he spotted two gray squirrels scampering around the pear tree, consumed by some insane mating ritual that looked as if it would continue forever. He smiled at their antics and thought: *I know how you feel.*

"Heads up," he called out. "Hot stuff coming through."

Amanda propped the pillows against the headboard, and he put the tray between them on the bed. He poured coffee into the mugs and before he handed one to her added two sugar cubes and a drop of milk. As she took the mug, she murmured: "I think I could get used to this."

They leaned against the pillows, sipping their coffee and munching on the chunks of brownie. Floyd entered the room, licking his lips after consuming his own breakfast. This picture of them all together seemed so right and felt so good to Carpo that he tossed his arms around Amanda and squeezed her.

"Ouch, Carpo!" She twisted away from him. "Watch out for my head."

"It still hurts?"

"A little." She patted the back of her head. "Actually, it's much better this morning. Last night I had a roaring headache."

"You should have woken me up."

"No, you were sleeping like a baby. Besides, what could you have done?"

"I don't know, found you some aspirin or something." He squeezed her hand. "How you feeling otherwise?"

"Okay, I guess." She shrugged. "I mean, no matter what, he was my father. I don't really know how I should feel about that."

He set down his mug. "Want to talk about it?"

"What do you want to know?"

"I guess, what happened. All I know still is that I came home and found you knocked out in the closet. I don't know what happened to you or how you even got there."

She shook her head, as if still in shock. "Good old Dad put me there," she said. "We were out in the driveway arguing and he tried to hit me. That's the last thing I remember. I must have fallen and knocked my head."

"Why were you in the driveway?"

"I was trying to stop him from driving to Trent Donovan's house."

"So it was after I called here?"

She nodded. "You're probably wondering about that too. When Dad first came over here, he was asking for you. He wouldn't tell me why, until he asked if I knew where Trent lived. Right there I knew he'd done it. I started screaming at him, calling him names and it was like, whammo, he snapped on me. He pulled that knife out and told me he was going to cut me. That's when you called. He made me answer the telephone and pretend that Mr. Donovan had called for you so he could get the address."

"And then you hit your head?"

"No, I ran after him, trying to stop him from getting in his car. He tried to punch me, and I must have slipped and gotten bopped on the noggin."

"Were you unconscious the entire time?"

"I think so. I don't remember anything until that ambulance arrived to help the guy you nailed."

"It's funny, but when I was at Mr. Donovan's cabin and opened the door, as soon as I saw your dad I felt totally at peace. It all made sense to me, like a puzzle fitting together. Finally, I knew who had killed Jack."

"You knew it was my dad?"

"No, nothing that strong, it just made sense. I remembered how you said that he lived in the area and hated Jack.

I might have guessed it even sooner if I'd known he was a state trooper." Carpo shifted onto his elbow. "Tell me what else you know. Like how the power and telephone lines got cut to the cottage, or how your car was moved."

"I guess my father drove the car to my house and then walked back here for his own car."

"That would explain why it took him so long to get to Trent Donovan's cabin after I gave you the address."

"Maybe. And as far as the power and telephone lines, I have no idea how they got cut. It happened after my own lights were out."

"Trooper Walker thinks Claudell Jenkins cut them. He found Claudell's car parked in a driveway on Beach Hill Road. He must have walked over from there, stopped, and cut the lines, then he probably hid in the woods until I got home."

"And he was really working with my dad?"

"According to Trooper Walker, he confessed to it at the hospital yesterday. They're a pretty unlikely pair, but it almost worked. They almost pulled it off."

Carpo took a sip of coffee: "That's one of the reasons I doubted you, Amanda. The night we had dinner at your house, you acted so strange when I asked if you had ever heard of Southville. Then I saw that painting of the doorway in the barn, and I remembered that Elizabeth Jessup heard that the folktale came from Southville. I didn't know what to think."

"I'm sorry about that, it was a totally instinctual response. My father hated that he came from that town. He ingrained it in my head never to admit it."

"And I assume that's how you knew about the doorway legend?"

"No, I really did learn that from Bethie. When I was growing up, I used to sneak down to the marina once a week to have tea with her. She used to talk about it, I guess it was a big deal if you grew up there. My father obviously knew about it, otherwise he wouldn't have tried to mimic it in all of the murders. He must have known the psychological impact it would have on the survivors."

He started to speak, but she held up her hand. "This might sound terrible, Michael, but I'm going to say it anyway. I'm glad he's dead. I feel like an incredible burden is off my shoulders. All these years I've been listening to him spit venom, hating everyone who came from that town. I can't believe how much he hated."

Suddenly, the question Carpo was about to ask didn't seem important anymore. They picked up their coffee mugs and drank in silence, lost in thought about all that had passed in Bridgewater that week. After a bit she said: "So what do you want to do on your last day?"

"I've still got some packing to do, and I think I should at least make an effort to sort through some of Jack's things before the house is sold. He was so good to me, I feel like I owe it to him."

She tossed her head back, the hair flying off her forehead. "It's not right to sell this place. I can't imagine anyone else living here, or at least anyone who's not an artist. Someone should turn this place into a writer's colony or a spiritual retreat."

"There's not much we can do about it, unless you have a spare couple of hundred thousand dollars lying around."

"Fat chance. So, what time will you hit the road tomorrow?"

"I've got to be at the newsroom by three for a meeting, so I'll probably leave here about eleven. I need some time to return the rental car and drop my bags and Floyd off at the apartment. Boy, is he in for a rude awakening."

"Poor Floyd," she gushed at the black lump of fur next to the bed. "No more chasing squirrels for you, you're a city dog now."

Floyd's tail thumped the floor as he recognized his name.

Amanda looked at Carpo, the smile on her face a poor mask for the seriousness of her eyes. "So I guess that means tonight's our last night."

"I'm afraid so."

"And will that be it? Will I ever see you again?"

He smiled as he reached for her face, rubbing his fingers lightly on her cheek. "Amanda, I'd walk through hell in a gasoline suit if it meant getting to see you again."

She grasped the belt of his robe and slowly undid it. "I'm going to hold you to that promise, but first we'll have to get you out of this robe, slip you into something a little more flammable."

They stayed in bed for another hour, making love, sipping lukewarm coffee, talking, cuddling, and then making love again. Floyd seemed quite bored with the display, emitting several loud groans and protesting whines. Afterward, they showered together and dressed, then shared another cup of coffee on the porch. Before she left they agreed to meet that evening to spend their last night together.

After she had gone, he packed his duffel bag with clothes

and the few nonperishable foods worth saving from the kitchen. He took one of the stubbies from the fridge, figuring that he would display it on his bookshelf in New York, perhaps the first object in his own collection of *chotchkes*.

When he had finished packing, he walked through the cottage, admiring the hundreds of objects and artifacts that collectively embodied the spirit of Jack Crawford. He looked at the photographs on the wall, flipped through the books, and inspected a few of the treasured letters. There was simply too much; too much to pack or even begin to catalogue. He decided to leave it as it was, and allow the new owner, whoever it may be, to decide what to do with everything. He hoped it would be someone who respected the previous owner.

In the end he chose three things besides the stubby to bring back to New York. He took the black-lacquer-framed photograph of Jack in his U.S. Navy uniform, face beaming with youth and determination. He also took the *forcola* that had saved his life two nights earlier. And finally, he took the Dale Carnegie–covered edition of *Sexus* by Henry Miller, complete with its underlined passages and airline ticket memory marker.

Before he placed the book in the duffel, he flipped through the pages and found the passage Jack had recited to him four years earlier. He read the words again now, felt their power anew, the simple message that every human is capable of uttering "profound truths" if only they have the confidence in their choices and their creative impulses.

Rusty brakes squeaked in the driveway. Carpo shoved the book into his duffel and walked to the kitchen to see who had arrived. His melancholy dissipated as soon as he spotted Trent Donovan's Toyota parked beside his car. He shouted a greeting from the door, then walked outside to see if he could help the man get out of his car.

Trent lumbered from the low front seat, his metal walker creaking as it accepted the burden of his weight. Carpo made a motion to help, but froze when a scowl passed over Trent's face. "For chrissakes, get out of my way. I may be a cripple, but I'm not totally helpless."

Carpo smiled. "And a good morning to you too, Mr. Donovan."

"Quit standing there ogling me. Run on inside and put on a pot of coffee."

He jogged to the kitchen, dumped out the old coffee, and started a fresh pot. The brown liquid was just beginning to splatter the carafe by the time Trent reached the screen door.

"Can I get that for you?" he offered when he saw Trent struggling to get his walker through the door.

He could tell that Trent wanted to snap at him, but he simply couldn't manage the door. He nodded silently, waiting for Carpo to hold open the door; then he carefully slid into the kitchen.

"Ah, yes," Trent murmured once he was inside, "Jack's favorite room. I remember when he raised the ceiling in here to make it a cathedral. We used to sit at that butcher block late into the night on Saturdays, sneaking pulls off a bourbon bottle while our wives was out gossiping on the porch."

There was enough coffee in the pot, so Carpo poured two mugs. "Mr. Donovan, how do you take your coffee?"

"Black," he snapped as if it were a foolish question. "And

what the hell's with all this Mr. Donovan business? Like I'm ninety or something. Call me Trent."

Carpo carried the mugs into the living room, sitting on the couch while Trent trudged in from the kitchen. When he made it there, he sat on the couch and pulled a white handkerchief from his pocket, which he dabbed across his forehead and nose. He sampled the coffee, gave an approving grunt to the taste, then stared out the bay windows. His brown eyes lost focus as he looked down at the murky blue waters of Lake Lillinonah.

After a minute of silence he said, "I suppose you'll be heading back to the city soon."

"Tomorrow morning."

"What time?"

"About eleven."

"Packed yet?"

"Just about."

Floyd ambled over to Trent and plopped an oversized paw in his lap. Carpo thought Trent would shoo the dog away, but instead he lovingly patted the dog's head, scratching him behind the ears.

"And what's going to happen to this damn fool dog?" Trent asked.

"He's coming with me. There's not a lot of room in my apartment, but I'll try to make it work. I just can't give him up to strangers."

"No, I'd think not," Trent said quietly. "When are you planning to visit Bridgewater again?"

"I don't know. Now that Jack's gone and his house is being sold, I think it might be a while before I get back. I will come back though. Someday."

Trent raised his eyes from the dog. He studied Carpo for a moment, as if he were about to ask a favor of him. At one point he started to say it, mouth opening, eyes widening, but then he stopped. Instead, he asked, "So when do you head back to work?"

"Tomorrow afternoon. Three o'clock sharp." Carpo rolled his eyes. "I feel like I just left there."

"Don't be grumbling there, Carpo. Before you know it you'll be my age, hobbled by a walker and wishing you could have another shot at youth."

Trent sipped his coffee, eyes spying Carpo over the rim of the mug, contemplating something again. Carpo considered asking him if something was bothering him, but decided to let it come on its own. Finally, it did.

"I have a little proposition to run past you, son, but I don't want you to respond until I finish laying the whole thing out. It occurred to me yesterday what a damn shame it'd be to let some stranger move into this place. They'd probably box up all of this crap and cart it to the dump. Most of it belongs there anyway, but the thing is, Jack's been collecting it for years and I'm afraid he'll come back from the grave and torment me if I let it happen. So here's what I'm thinking of: I placed a call to Athens, Georgia, this morning and had a chat with Jack's sister about buying the place. I'll be coming into that lease money soon enough and, well, I'd like it very much if you'd come up here and stay at the place. Maybe you could dust Jack's junk once in a while and tend to his gardens. I'll give you your own set of keys and you don't have to worry about calling, just show up whenever you find the time. It'd make me feel better,

Carpo, 'cause I know how much Jack loved you, like you were one of his own. He would've wanted it this way."

Carpo nearly yelped, the happiness burst so hard inside of him. "Mr. Donovan, I mean Trent, oh, my God, thank you. I won't bother you at all, I promise. You won't even know I'm in the same house as you."

"Hell are you talking about?" Trent snorted. "I've lived in a shack my entire life, why would I want to live in this place. No, sir, I'm buying myself a real home, one of those big white colonials that sits up on Route 133. Figure it's about time this town got a little flavor of Southville in it."

Carpo spent the remainder of the afternoon puttering around the cottage, getting it ready for his departure. He straightened and threw white sheets over the furniture, then he dusted and pulled the blinds. He looked at the place in a different light now, especially since he knew that it wouldn't be the last time he'd ever see it.

Despite the kind offer by Trent Donovan, he still had a hollow feeling in his gut. The sun was plummeting on the opposite side of the valley and, as he stepped out to the patio, it occurred to him that his vacation was ending just as fast. In little more than twelve hours it would be time to head back to the city, and back to the mania of Channel 8. He didn't feel as though he'd ever been on vacation.

There was a cool breeze blowing across the yard that smelled, he thought, strongly of fall. He had never visited the cottage during a time when he could use the fireplace; he imagined what it would feel like to sit in the living room with a fire spitting and crackling in the hearth.

Maybe I'll start that book about Jack, he thought, *and try to do something as permanent as he did.*

He walked back inside the house to the telephone in the living room. Without even thinking about it, he picked up the phone and dialed the number from heart. He'd been thinking of the number all week. As the phone started to ring, his heart began pounding so hard and fast that he almost felt as though he would faint.

How long has it been? he wondered. *Four years? Or is it already five?*

The phone rang half a dozen times without an answer. Just as he started to hang up, a painfully familiar voice came on the line and said, "Hello?"

"Hi," Carpo said, cringing at the crack-ups in his voice. He had never been so nervous in his life.

"Who is this?"

"It's me, Michael." He paused for a second, wondering if the line had gone dead. Then he heard breathing, and he knew he was still there. "How are you? I've really missed you."